9 780441 736966

50395

SORCERY AND ADVENTURE! THE EPIC NEW SERIES!

RuneSword

Volume Three
THE DREAMSTONE

J.F. Rivkin

Cal was surrounded, orcs all around him. His sword flashed in the starlight. The orcs fell back before him, their red eyes wide in the blackness. Each time the glittering sword bit home there were squealing sounds, and a pair of red eyes would shut.

The sight of blood increased his frenzy, and Cal hacked his way through his enemies. He was as bold and merciless as a thunderstorm in the mountains. Before him, he saw the creatures kneeling—whether in supplication or death, it mattered not. Their passing was of no importance. There was a screaming in his ears.

Endril watched him, and for all his peril, he gaped. The boy was possessed, it was clear. Then there was a blow, and Endril fell to the ground, borne down by an orc. The orc grinned, revealing sharp yellow fangs. He bent low, ready to bite out his captive's throat . . .

*Books in the RUNESWORD Series
from Ace*

RUNESWORD VOLUME ONE: OUTCASTS
RUNESWORD VOLUME TWO: SKRYLING'S BLADE
RUNESWORD VOLUME THREE: THE DREAMSTONE

RUNESWORD VOLUME FOUR: HORRIBLE HUMES
(Coming in July)

Volume Three
THE DREAMSTONE

J.F. Rivkin

ACE BOOKS, NEW YORK

THE DREAMSTONE

CHAPTER
1

They rode through the lush autumn countryside, past isolated cottages and farms that were lost in the vast sweeps of land surrounding them. They saw no one. Only groups of cows and horses watched them, with impassive and unreflective eyes, as they passed.

The road curved and dipped, then rose again as it took them higher into the foothills. At times, surprising vistas opened before them, and the jagged spine of mountains became visible: Towering over them all was Mount Thalia. Snowcapped and aloof, a solitary cone of ice and snow, it seemed a concrete symbol of hidden worlds—worlds of mystery, power, and loneliness.

It was late afternoon and the sun, low in the sky, spilled its molten light over the peaks, while the moon, coming into the ascendant, cast its pure, cold eye over the land. To Elizebith, it seemed that every voice in the world was stilled, and that she too, for once a member of the harmony, had achieved a moment of serenity. She wondered how long it would last.

As if on cue, Cal cleared his throat. The crystalline land of light and silence, impossibly fragile, shattered. Bith was thrust back into everyday life. Before she could stop herself, a sigh escaped her.

"Problem, princess?" Cal asked. His voice was light and cheerful. Whatever reveries had occupied him, they had been pleasant.

Bith studied his face for a moment before replying. It was a good face, she thought, plain and honest, and open. The scar that ran from lip to chin no longer bothered her—it was a part of him as much as his blue eyes or pug nose. Cal, with his tousled hair and endearing smile, always made her think of a little cottage she had once stayed in. Humble in appearance but solidly built and with a blazing fire within, it had sheltered her well from foul weather and danger.

Cal too, she thought, had a fire within him, and she also thought that some of its flame might burn for her. There had been times, especially since her rescue from Murcroft's tower, when he had seemed unusually gentle and tender.

Bith hadn't tried to encourage Cal. He had a place in her heart, but more as the brother she'd longed for since she was a child than as the lover she'd daydreamed about as she grew older. He, Endril, and Hathor were her family. Safe harbors in a world that teemed with dangers and uncertainty. She smiled wryly. A disgraced squire, a banished elf, and a vegetarian troll—she'd heard of odd families, but surely there were few to match hers.

"Um, are you with us, Bith?" Cal asked.

"Oh, I'm sorry . . . I was daydreaming."

"And so was I—of a bright fire, roasted meat, and a soft bed. What of you?"

"I don't know. Nothing, really."

He grinned. "Try my daydreams—they're more interesting. Particularly the roasted meat part—roast venison, flavored with sage and mint, is one of the most intriguing thoughts in the world."

"It is a profound subject," Endril declared.

"You see, even Endril agrees with me," Cal said. "How often does that happen?"

"I do not agree with you. I was commenting on the subject of nothingness. It is worth a lifetime of reflection."

Cal snorted. "Maybe your lifetime, but not mine. I'd rather think of other things—good food, strong ale, glory in battle. And even better than thinking is doing. Dreams make an insubstantial meal, at best." He paused and rubbed his stomach. "Speaking of meals—when do we eat? It's been hours since we stopped. Is there an inn anywhere about this forsaken place?"

Endril nodded. "A few miles down the road. We'll reach it before darkness falls." He turned to Bith. "What were your thoughts, if I do not intrude?"

Bith hesitated. "I'm not sure I can explain." She shifted nervously in her saddle. Endril, with his lean, hollow-cheeked face and intense eyes, always seemed to know more about her than she did herself. He seemed to know more about anything than anyone else. Giving him satisfactory answers could be a trying experience. Elves, she thought, were not the easiest companions.

"I wasn't thinking of anything, really. Everything was so quiet. I was quiet. There was just the mountains and the light . . . and . . . and—" She stopped, frustrated at her inability to explain herself.

But Endril seemed satisfied. "They are precious, these moments of transcendence. And all too fleeting. They exist in a place where words are superfluous. To attempt to describe them is futile. There are some few who, having tasted them, then spend their lives searching for a path which leads to them unerringly and without fail. It is a difficult quest. Some would say an impossible one."

"Have they succeeded?" Bith asked.

"Perhaps a few. But how can we tell? Silence is the keystone of that realm. Certainly it is a treacherous road, and dragons watch at the gate."

"Then you'd best take me with you, Bith," Cal broke in. "Dragons, as we all know, are my specialty." He pulled his sword and brandished it over his head.

"Ha, dragons are fierce," said Hathor. "They breathe hot like the sun, and their hearts are cold." He spoke slowly and carefully, his speech a mirror of his thinking. "They love gold and blood." He smiled widely, showing his fangs. "Once I saw one. It was very beautiful. It ate a troll."

Bith groaned. "How charming. Besides, we've all seen a dragon." She shuddered. "It was not at all like the sun, and it certainly was not beautiful—it was black and stinking and horrid. What are you talking about?"

"Those are the Dark Lord's children—special to him, bred by him for his own. They are black, like his heart. These others are free and wild. They care for nothing—not even the Evil One himself." With his stubby fingers, the troll made a sign, a protective gesture used by his people when they mentioned the Dark Lord. "But the real dragons—oh, very pretty." He flapped his thick arms up and down in an imitation of flight. "Like birds on fire."

"That's for me," Cal said, stabbing at the air. "Under the belly like so . . . " He thrust his sword up. "And then split it from the gut to the gizzard. Killing wild dragons sounds glorious."

"You're so brave," said Bith.

Cal bowed his head. "Thank you, madam. I will not deny that which is so clearly true."

"And would you dare such a feat without an enchanted blade?" she said teasingly. "That sword has no magic about it."

"No? Was it not given to me by King Grimnison in

gratitude for killing the beast of the sea? Was it not a great deed, and have not the minstrels of the Skrisung composed a song about it which they sing in their mead halls? Will not their children learn this song and sing of it to their own children in turn?''

Hathor sighed. "It was a mighty song—it had many, many verses.''

Cal looked lovingly at the sword, which glittered in the daylight. Engraved along its length were runes, and on the pommel was the figure of a warrior bestriding a fallen monstrosity. He sheathed it slowly.

"Forgive me," Bith said. "I spoke without thinking.''

Cal waved his hand lightly, a picture of lordly benevolence. She giggled.

Cal began to sing at the top of his lungs:

> The halls of the king lay silent,
> For doom was upon the land.
> Mercy had fled from its borders,
> And death stood near at hand.

"Of course, she is still little more than a child," Endril muttered, totally oblivious to Cal's noise. "Quite unprepared for such an important decision.''

They all turned to him. "I beg your pardon," Bith said in a haughty voice. "To whom are you referring?" Cal rolled his eyes at Hathor.

"To you, of course," Endril replied. "You are very young, and have much time to decide what path to take. Better now that you acquire experience, so that should you ever consider the journey, the scales will be fairly weighted. There is much to be said for the world, both good and bad. You are, as yet, still unschooled in its many ways.''

"There's one for you, Lady Know-It-All," Cal said and laughed.

Bith tossed her head, throwing back her long black hair. Her silver eyes flashed. "I've never pretended to know more than I do, I'm sure." Cal sniggered. Pointedly, she ignored him. "Still, I don't think I'm as raw as you make out. I'm hardly a green girl anymore."

"Right now, you're certainly behaving like one," Endril replied.

Bith gritted her teeth, trying to get a rein on her temper. She failed miserably. Endril was simply too keen on pointing out everyone's lack of knowledge. Everyone's but his, of course.

"Speaking of path," she said sharply, "you haven't mentioned why you were so insistent we take this one. It's not the liveliest spot I've ever seen—or the warmest. And whatever the reason," she muttered under her breath, "it's probably unpleasant." Cal winked at her. He'd heard her last comment quite clearly, as had Hathor and Endril. She had, of course, fully intended that.

"I've come in search of someone."

"You mean we've come. And since we are plainly becoming involved in something, perhaps you'd deign to tell us what it is—if you think our feeble intellects can comprehend it."

The elf sighed. "I hadn't wanted to bring it up so soon, but since you are quite insistent, I'll explain. I'm looking for a sorceress who supposedly lives in these mountains. Somewhere on Mount Thalia."

"Somewhere?" asked Cal, in a despairing tone.

"Where is somewhere?" Hathor said. "Is it far? I am very hungry."

"It's east of the sun and west of the moon," Bith snapped.

"Get used to being hungry." An expression of deep sadness came over the troll's face.

Cal looked over at him. "Been dreaming about turnips?" he asked, his voice dripping with sympathy.

"Endril, have you ever met this woman?" Bith demanded.

"No, and I'm not sure she's still in this country. She may have left, she may be dead, she may never have existed. There are many possibilities." Endril seemed to regard this as favorable.

Hathor's depression deepened.

"You're a real comfort," "Bith said. "Why are you so anxious to chase this phantasm?"

"Because she would be useful to us, of course."

"Of course! You're a bold one, you are! What right do you have to drag us out here without a by-your-leave? And for what? So we can learn some exciting new ways to risk our lives? No, thank you." She paused for breath. "Is this some scheme of that pompous, lying, worst excuse for a lawful and supposedly beneficent immortal I ever hope to see, Vili?"

"No."

Bith closed her eyes in exasperation. "Then this is strictly your own affair. Why have you dragged us into it?"

"Surely we have a duty to learn all we can of the Dark Lord's plots. I have no doubt that this land will shortly fall under his scrutiny. Rumors have already reached me that he is testing its borders. We can ignore nothing that may aid us in his final defeat—even if the task is difficult."

Cal pricked up his ears. "That's right, princess. Besides, fortune and glory are nothing to sneer at." His eyes shone. "I have yet to use this sword in battle."

"Surely I have the right to make my own decisions about these things?" Bith's face was flushed and the light dappling of freckles across her nose stood out clearly. Cal thought she looked lovely.

"We should do what is good," Hathor said quietly. He stroked his horse's mane. Disagreements always made him nervous and uncertain. Cal's teasing nature and Bith's fiery temper were constant puzzles to him. He had long since stopped trying to understand Endril. Hathor knew there were some things that were bound to remain mysteries.

"I'm tired of being noble," Bith continued in a sulky tone. "Nobility seems to mean danger and dirt. I remember all those romances I read when I dwelt with my mother. There were dangers, certainly. But, as I recall, the princess sat in a golden tower, or an ivory palace, and waited for the handsome knight to rescue her. There were always servants and dainties on silver trays, and some ridiculous tale of a worm, or an ogre, or an evil magician. But they were really quite agreeable fellows, ready to lie down and die almost as soon the gallant hero trotted up on his steed. There was absolutely no mention of squalor, misery, and terror. Besides"—and here her voice took on a harsher tone—"I don't hold with sorceresses."

"So speaks the fair enchantress herself," Cal hooted.

"You understand what I mean," Bith retorted. "We've had no good luck with magicians, as you well know."

"Now, princess, keep faith with your own kind. After all, you are a magician yourself—maybe not a very good one . . ."

"Oh, is that so? And who opened up the cavern? And who added a few inches to your puny height? And, speaking of competence, it seems to me I remember a little contest between you and that Skrisung warrior . . . what was his name?" She wrinkled her brow. "You know, it was after your last trip to the wine cellar, when you said you got lost, and . . ."

"That was quite a different matter," Cal said, clearing his throat. "That was merely a friendly contest, not a matter of life and death. How was I to know that was his wife?" He rubbed his jaw. "She didn't act like it."

"Oh, I'm *so* sorry," Bith said, giving him her sweetest smile. "It certainly looked like life and death for you, but again, I must have been mistaken. I suppose the dicing game you had with that crooked dealer two towns back . . . "

"What!" he roared. "Crooked! And you knew and didn't say anything?"

"Well, as I recall, you said that being a sheltered little princess, I wouldn't understand games of chance the way you did and if anyone cheated you, you'd have his head. But I clearly remember that the gentleman left with his head quite firmly on his shoulders and three of your gold coins quite decidedly in his pouch. I took it as an act of charity on your part. You don't mean to say"—and her eyes widened in a parody of amazement—"that you thought he was honest?"

Endril spurred his horse ahead of them. "Did I say you were behaving like a green girl?" he said as he passed. "Forgive me. I was incorrect. Both of you are behaving like nursery brats."

CHAPTER 2

Galen's Hearth was just the sort of inn one would expect to find in the back country. The usual row of tarnished mugs lined the wall. The air held the familiar tang of onions, smoke, and damp clothes drying. Long benches and tables were the only places to sit, and they carried the history of the inn on their surface—a dreary tale of spilled food and drink set there plain as day for any to read who had the stomach.

Huddled over their ale, small groups of farmers talked among themselves in low tones. Galen himself stared fixedly at some flies that were buzzing lazily around a crock of pickles. Occasionally, he flapped his dishcloth at them in a halfhearted gesture to chase them away. His heavy face was carved into a scowl. The lines around his mouth suggested that it was his habitual expression. The lines deepened when the four travelers stepped inside.

"Out!" he roared. Everyone in the inn looked up. The muttering rose a bit in volume.

"I beg your pardon?" Bith said in her most regal manner.

"Those two," Galen replied, shaking a finger at Endril and Hathor. "Out. We don't serve their kind here."

11

"Good sir," Endril said, "what is the trouble?"

"There's no trouble, if you leave. Stay, and you'll learn what trouble is," Galen retorted. "Haven't we had enough misery in these parts without inviting what ain't human into our homes?" Bith cast her eyes about the room and sniffed.

Cal stepped forward, his face flushed. "These are our friends. We don't stay if they don't."

"Suits me. You know where the door is."

"Do you have any idea who we are?" Cal demanded. "We are the heroes of Cairngorm, the repellers of the Mistwall. I personally slew the bane of the Skrisung—a horrible monster with thirteen eyes, eleven mouths, and twoscore and two arms. The evil magician Murcroft met his defeat at our hands."

"Never heard of you," said Galen. Reluctantly, he drew his attention from the flies to look at Cal more closely. "You don't look like much of a warrior. You look more like the boy who blacks boots to me. Now, young master, as I was saying, the door is . . ."

"Oh, Galen, let them stay." An old man, rather poorly clad, had stood up. His face was ruddy, partly from the light of the fire, partly from the ale he had drunk.

"Hold your besotted tongue, John Sillar," Galen said.

Sillar ignored him. "The lad is a glorious liar, and this place is as dull tonight as your old woman's bed." He laughed loudly at his own wit. "And besides," he continued, "we can't turn a young lady out into the night." He bowed low to Bith, and gave her a charming smile. Then he staggered and fell heavily against a table. The farmers seated there barely looked up. Sillar took one of the mugs from the table, held it out in a toast to Bith, and downed it. "Your health, madam," he said.

"Why," Bith whispered to Endril, "are we trying so hard to stay in a place which is barely fit for pigs? I, for one, would be more than glad to do the landlord's bidding. Spending the night amidst drunkards and peasants holds no appeal.''

"We either stay here or we sleep on the ground. It is the only inn for many miles, and I think it may be unsafe to remain outdoors at night," the elf answered. "A word, Galen," he said, turning toward the landlord, who stepped back hurriedly, knocked into the already unsteady Sillar, and fell over backwards on top of him. The hapless fellow lay underneath Galen, groaning.

"Oh, mother, I'm killed," Sillar cried, as if in great agony. "You tub of guts, get your backside off me. Someone get me a drink, for I'm dying."

Endril reached down and hauled Galen to his feet. He talked to him too quietly for the rest of them to hear, but the flash of gold in his hand was plain. At first, Galen was adamant, shaking his head back and forth like an apple tossed about in a strong wind. There was a chinking sound, as of coin against coin, and the strong wind quieted to a gentle breeze. One more coin, and the breeze died away completely.

Endril returned to his companions. "We may stay the night."

"Oh, joy," said Bith.

They sat together in a corner of the room, staring at their meal. Cal considered using his sword to cut the meat, which was as dry and tough as a stick of wood, but thought better of it: It was too great a risk—he might damage the blade.

Bith tried nibbling at a piece of bread, but tossed it down in disgust. It made a clearly audible clatter. Endril sipped at his ale and stared at the wall, lost in his own dreams. Only Hathor seemed happy. He hummed tunelessly as he ate, shoveling bread and vegetables hungrily into his mouth.

Looking up in surprise, he said, "Why no eat? Must keep up strength." He offered Bith a rather withered carrot.

She smiled faintly and took it. "I'll save it for later."

Hathor shook his head. "Not wise, lady. Eat when the food is there. Is the only meal can be sure of."

"Now then, my friends," said a cheery voice. It was John Sillar. "Enjoying our meal? Ready for some good talk?" He sat down next to Cal. "Why, there's a fine roast you've got there, master." He eyed the meat greedily.

"Help yourself," Cal said, offering him the carving knife.

"You're a generous lad," Sillar returned, and hacked off a chunk for himself. He pulled a piece of bread off the loaf and wiped the meat over it. "Gets more flavor that way," he told Bith. "You should try it."

"I'll keep it in mind," she said, wrinkling her nose. She moved her chair a bit back from the table.

Sillar turned his attention to Hathor. "Hey there, my friend, do you eat nothing but the green stuff? With teeth like yours, I'd think something more substantial would be to your taste. You *are* a troll, are you not?"

Hathor nodded. "Oh, yes, very old troll family."

"From what I've heard, trolls are flesh-eaters. Not averse to a bit of the long pig, if you take my meaning."

"I am changing that. Eat vegetables only."

Sillar clucked his tongue. "Imagine that, now. I've fallen in with a reformer. Only vegetables. Sounds dreary to me. Not against the drink, are you?"

"No, no. Drink is very good." To prove his point, Hathor refilled his mug from the pitcher on the table. He then took Bith's mug, which she hadn't used, and filled it too. He shoved it over to Sillar, who raised it high.

"To your good health, and a safe and fortunate journey." He downed the brew in a few gulps.

"What is your trade, Master Sillar?" Endril asked. "Do you come from these parts?"

"Why, where I come from, good sir, is the great land of Here-and-There. And my trade is whatever's at hand. Do you need some wood chopped? Then Sillar's your man. When your blood tells you spring's at hand and lambing time's near, look for me! I've no objection to hard work, so long as there's an end to it. And when I've done my job, I'm off—leaving it all behind me—the good and the bad, the sorrows, the troubles, the joys. No man has a claim on me, nor no woman neither—though a few have tried." He winked at Bith.

Pointing at his clothes, he said, "As you see, I'm not the richest of men. But I'm a happy one, and how many can make that claim? I'm over fifty, and still not bored with the world and its ways. It's an endless story to me, and I'm always looking for the next part to the tale. As for its ending"—he shrugged—"it comes when it comes."

"You are a philosopher," Endril said.

"Perhaps you'd say so, sir. Though many have called me much worse than that." He leaned closer to Endril. "But my true work is that of gossip. It's why I stepped in with that sour Galen. When I saw you unlikely four wander into this place, and when I heard this stout lad come out with his bag of tales, then I knew I'd found something truly valuable."

He flung his arms wide, as if to gather up the entire room with all its occupants, and bring them close to him.

"These poor folks—what do they know of the world? They're tied to their bits of land, and most of them go no further than a trip to the fair each fall. I'm a blessing to them—a piece of the mysterious places that lie outside their ken. This boy's stories will earn me many a night's lodging this winter."

"Stories!" Cal broke in. "I told no stories. We are who I said . . . the heroes of Cairngorm. This is Endril the elf, and this is Hathor. Here sits the Lady Elizebith, and I am named Caltus Talienson. No man calls me a liar!"

Sillar regarded him calmly, a small smile on his lips. "Fiery, aren't you? Stuffed to the gills with noble deeds and hopes, I'll wager. And you've done what you say? Well, it's a fine, brave life you're leading. But whether it's true or no, it's of little matter to me, or those I'll be talking to."

"How can you say that?" Cal demanded. "Have you no regard for the truth?"

Sillar shrugged his shoulders. "No, not anymore. I used to—when I was your age. Although what I meant by it, I'm sure I don't know. I think, by truth, you mean facts—your facts. These people are well acquainted with facts—for their faces are rubbed into them every day. Facts hem them in every which way they turn. It is not facts they want to hear from me, no matter their origin." He laughed. "And why are you so anxious that they know it's real?"

Cal blushed. "I told you—because it's true."

"Oh, aye, that's part of it, I don't doubt. And maybe there's just a bit of pride mixed in?"

"Great deeds should be sung about," Cal retorted. "There is no shame in glory, honestly won. Already, songs have been composed about my deeds."

"Well, my young hero, you're no different than the rest of us in that regard. We all need to feel our place in the world, whether we're farmers or warriors. And none of us mind being thought a bit worse than we are. Why, when I talk to these folk in the bitter winter nights, you should hear the tales they tell. They don't hold me on oath when I talk to them, and I return the courtesy."

"What can farmers know of brave deeds?" Cal said, a

bit of scorn in his voice. "Surely they must talk of giant cabbages, and hens that lay perfect eggs?"

Sillar hooted. "Oh, to be your age again, eh, Master Endril?" He nudged the elf in the ribs.

"Do you know what they talk about? Not hens or cabbages, I promise you. It's all what great lovers they are, the beautiful women they've bedded, the seducers they were in their youth, the terrible and glorious fights they've been in.

"A woman, who's never known but a single man in all her life will whisper to me, after he's abed, of the other men she's known—and all of them are princes or knights, like yourself. The exact opposite of her husband, who stinks of sweat and garlic, and puts his dirty feet on her backside during the cold winter nights.

"These simple people, who've no more done anything so daring than I've flown to the moon, are as full of such stories as an egg is of meat. And to them those stories are truth. Oh, they're not mad. They know full well that those things haven't really happened to them. But they're telling me their dreams, dreams that speak of some part of themselves that goes beyond cabbages and hens and dirt. Do you see? It's their way of saying, 'Look, here is the rest of me, the part that's been hidden by grime and toil. I cannot rest until someone knows that I am greater than I seem. Do not let me go to my grave without letting the world know what I truly am.' "

Cal shrugged. "I *don't* see. Truth to me is what I've done—what I can feel or taste or smell. I *have* killed monsters, and been in battles. These other people—well, I think they sound like liars. It's as simple as that."

Sillar shook his head. "Have it your own way. I've long ago given up arguing with folk about anything but the price of an ale. You're too young yet, perhaps, to have regrets and lost hopes.''

Cal snorted in disgust.

"Master Sillar," said Endril, "ply your trade with us. We have need of the sort of tales you bear. What has been happening here that make the people so suspicious?''

Sillar took a long pull at his ale. ''Now, there's a question. Begging your leave, but part of it is your leaf-eating companion, the troll.''

Hathor looked up at him in surprise.

"Though this fellow seems gentle enough, you must see that folks are leery of someone who looks upon them as I look upon this roast here.''

Hathor shook his head in protest and waved a turnip. "Only these I eat. No meat.''

"Ah, but no one can be expected to know that, can they? Perhaps you should wear a sign. Still, it's more than that. Strange things have been happening, my friends. There can be no doubt. The world is changing, and not for the good.''

"In what way?'' Endril asked.

"The truth—or the facts, as my young friend would have it—is that a bit further on the land has changed. It's gone grey and dead, as though winter had already laid a cold hand upon it. It's too early in the year for that. I have seen it myself. And odd folk have been lurking in the mountains. Although I can't prove it, I swear I've spied shadows where there should be none, and shapes that seemed''—he hesitated—''*wrong* is the only word I know for it. And others besides me have done the same.''

He looked at the four of them in turn. Seeing the intent look on their faces, he continued his tale. ''There are other things, harder to explain. At first it was the children, who would wake from their sleep screaming. Now, their parents have also been having dreams that are too terrible to talk

about. Nightmares filled with images of death and grief."
He paused and stared blankly for a moment, then shook his
head hard. "I have suffered those dreams. They are evil.
Even when I am awake, they return to torment me."

"Is there anything else you know?" Endril asked, his
voice gentle.

"No, not really. People talk of seeing faces in the clouds,
and, in pools, reflections that are not their own. I cannot
vouch for them—I have been spared those horrors." He
sighed deeply. "It's glad I am that I'm leaving these parts.
I have nothing here to hold me."

"Have you heard of a witch, a sorceress, who lives in
these parts?"

Sillar laughed. "Aye, who has not? Tales about her are
as common hereabouts as daisies in the fields."

"Have you seen her?"

"No, or not that I know. They say she can shift her shape
at will. I've heard her described as a fabulous beast, with
a woman's lovely breasts, the claws of an eagle, and the
face of a lion. Certainly I'd remember something like that."

He seemed to recall something, and his face twisted into
a wry grin.

"A few years back, some of the farmers said the witch
was on the prowl, chasing after the young bucks hereabouts.
They talked about meeting a lovely woman, always in the
evening, who said she was the Grey Sorceress. She was a
very . . . er"—he glanced nervously at Bith—"*friendly* sort
of witch, from the sound of it."

"Really," Bith said coldly, "you needn't make allow-
ances for me. I'm quite aware of what 'friendly' means."

"Oh, I'm sure, lady," Sillar said, raising a hand to his
mouth as if to wipe it, but really to hide the smile on his
face.

"As you can imagine, taking the night air became quite

a popular pastime. Some thought it odd that the witch would demand silver for her favors, for surely a sorceress could conjure money from the air. She said that she must have something silver in return for what she gave, or the magic would fail. It seemed fair enough to the lads. Of course, it turned out the girl was no sorceress at all but simply a young lady with a good head for business. Still, I suppose she was an enchantress, in her own way.''

He turned back to Endril. "If you truly seek this witch, then my best advice is to go to Mount Thalia, for all the stories say her dwelling is there. They also say that if you find her it will be by no will of your own. She will come to you, if she wishes. If she does not, then you will stumble about in circles until you abandon your quest.''

He looked searchingly at Endril, who returned his gaze without flinching. "You've a good face, friend elf, though marked by pride. It may be that's what set you wandering in the first place, eh? A stiff backbone has often been the cause of worn-out boots.''

"I may not speak of it,'' Endril said, and to those who knew him, his voice sounded shaken.

"Aye, I've no wish to pry. It's enough for me to feel that if you seek this woman, your purpose is for good and not for evil. What do *you* know of her?''

"Little,'' Endril replied, his composure returned. "She is spoken of in a few of our tales, but as someone far removed from the affairs of this world. I do not know if she is good or bad, or even if those terms have meaning for her.''

"And why do you seek her?''

"I look for her help. Your tales are true, friend Sillar. Danger threatens this land, for the Dark Lord is rising and stretching out his hand.''

"And you're the one to set it all right?'' Sillar asked.

"So he thinks," Bith said, "though he's asked none of us."

"And what do you say, lady?"

Bith shook her head. "I say I've ridden all day, that I'm weary, and that I wish to sleep. Those are the only things I can be certain of." She rose. "I will let you trade your tales. I have no wish to hear of dangers tonight. I fear that the beds in this place will be trial enough." With a stately bow of her head, she left them and went to Galen to inquire about her room.

They watched as, a moment later, she disappeared up the stairs, holding some blankets, led by a serving girl with a jug of water in one hand and a candle in the other. "Very beautiful," Sillar murmured. "A queen in the making.

"Now, Sir Caltus," he said more cheerfully, "tell us of these monsters."

The serving girl set down the jug and candle, curtseyed awkwardly, and left. Bith stared about her gloomily. The room was small and shabbily furnished with a chair, small table, and narrow bed. A cracked basin and a piece of rough toweling were on the table. Straw poked through the bed's mattress ticking.

From behind one of the walls came a small, insistent gnawing sound. It could mean only one thing—mice. Bith curled her lip in distaste. Crossing to the window, she threw open the shutters to let in the night air.

She leaned out and took a deep breath. Overhead, the constellations glittered. On the horizon, she could pick out the Knight and, to the right, his eternal foe, the Dragon. When these two claimed their rightful place in the sky, directly above, it would be winter.

She pulled her head back in and started making up the bed, first covering the mattress with her cloak, then peering closely at the two blankets. Satisfied that they were at least clean, she spread them out and smoothed down the wrinkles.

"If nothing else, I'd make a fair lady's maid," she muttered. "Oh yes, madame, I'm greatly experienced. Hovels, dungeons, dreary inns . . . I've stayed in them all and made them as clean and homelike as could be. No matter what your circumstances, you'll find I'm always ready to give satisfaction." Rummaging in her pack, she pulled out a brush, mirror, and plain white shift. She dropped a curtsey to the bed and sat on it.

Picking up the mirror, Bith stared intently at her face. Her reflection, with its strange silver eyes, stared back.

"Who are you?" she whispered. "What's to become of you? I want answers!" But her reflection had no answers to give. It simply mouthed her own questions back at her. Then she yawned. It looked so odd she couldn't help but laugh. She stuck her tongue out at herself.

"In your future," she said, in a slow, deep voice, "I see . . . sleep!"

She threw off her clothes and washed herself, shivering at the touch of the cold water, then drew on the shift. The blankets felt fine as she wrapped them about herself. She blew out the candle and waited for sleep.

From directly behind her the quiet gnawing continued. "Mouse," Bith said, in a menacing voice, "cease your noise or I, Elizebith, daughter of the dreaded sorceress Morea, will transform myself into a cat and devour you slowly. I have had nothing to appease my hunger this night." The gnawing continued. Angrily, she slammed her fist against the wall. "Quiet!" she shouted. There was a frantic scampering sound, and the gnawing stopped. The room was silent.

A moment later, Bith was asleep.

• • •

It was dark. Bith ran frantically through a wood, panting hard. Something was chasing her, something that lived in the darkness. She couldn't see it, but its hot breath was on her neck. Far ahead a light shimmered. If only she could reach it! But her movements were becoming sluggish, as though the air had thickened its substance, impeding her flight. The light quivered, as if about to go out.

Instead, it broadened its beam and grew more intense. The path beneath her feet was illuminated, and ahead was a small house. The light was a lamp burning in its window. "Please, please, let me in," she shouted as she reached the door. From behind, a hand, slippery and warm, crept around her waist. "Love me, love me," whispered a voice in her ear.

Frantically, she pounded at the door. It flew open and she was inside. The hand and voice were gone. Bith stood on the sill, gasping for breath.

"Hello, my dear. Shut the door." An old woman was looking at her kindly. Behind her, a large pot was on the hearth, sending up curls of steam.

"I was about to have some soup." The old woman turned away and bent over the fire. She began poking the coals with a long stick. "Rest with me awhile."

"Thank you." Bith sat at the table, and listened to the pounding of her heart. That, and the crackling of flames, were the only sounds. She felt dizzy. Her face was hot and prickly, as with the onset of fever. "Please . . . but . . . I'm lost," she said with difficulty. The words came off her thick tongue slowly and clumsily.

"You're safe here, Elizebith. This is where you belong."

"How do you know my name?"

The old woman turned. Her body uncoiled and became straight and graceful. Her face melted and ran like candle wax. The features reshaped themselves and Morea stood before her. The stick writhed in her hand and became a sword. There was blood along its length.

"Would I not know my own daughter, my image reborn?"

"No." Bith backed away, holding out her hands. "I am not you!"

Her mother stepped forward. "You were always willful and stubborn! How can you be so sure? Did you ever truly know me? Do you truly know yourself? Foolish girl!" She held the sword out. "Take it, it is for you. I have wrought the blade from my bones and tempered it with my blood."

"Get away," Bith screamed. "I hate you!" She swung wide with one arm and struck her mother in the face. There was a thumping sound and a shriek . . .

"Bith, are you all right?" Cal shouted. He was pounding on the door. "Let us in!"

Bith looked about, bewildered. She was standing up, beside the window. Her hand smarted, and the shutter swung back and forth on its hinges. It was almost dawn.

"Bith! Open the door!"

"Yes, yes, I'm coming. It's fine," she called. She hurried to the door and let them in. Cal grabbed her and held her. She rested against him for a moment, feeling safe and comforted.

"I'm sorry," she said, gently pulling away. "It was a nightmare."

Endril looked at her intently. "Will you tell us about it?"

Bith sat down on the bed and slowly recounted her dream. It was vivid in her memory. Her voice shook a bit as she spoke.

"All of us have dreamt of terrible things," Endril said.

"Hathor woke us up with his bellowing," Cal said, trying to smile. "None of us could sleep after that—we'd all been troubled. We decided to dress and get ready to leave. A bit later, we heard you. Do you think it was Galen's awful dinner? That food would upset anybody's stomach—even a troll's.''

"What did you dream about?" Bith asked.

Cal shook his head slowly. "I don't remember my dream as clearly as you do yours, but it was awful. I was in a terrible battle. The dead were piled a foot high, and the wounded lay among them, crying out. What a stench—it was unbelievable. It seemed like the end of the world. I was searching among the heaps, trying to find Sir Edric. From behind, I heard someone call my name so I turned around. It was him, standing there, but he was dead." Cal shuddered, and then went on. "A pike was stuck through his body, and blood was coming out of his nose and his mouth. He looked straight at me and pointed and said, 'Coward.' That's when I woke up."

Cal stopped. He seemed lost in his dreadful recollection. Bith touched him gently on the shoulder, and then turned to Hathor. "And you?"

"Blood for me too," Hathor answered. "And pictures of the dead behind my eyes. There were skulls and bones lying about, and a great fire. Something roasting on a spit. Voices crying in my ears . . . voices of murdered peoples."

For once, Bith was not impatient with Hathor's slowness of speech. She didn't want to hear a clearer description of his dream.

Hathor's voice started to shake. "I do not want these things. Why do they come to me in my sleep?" He looked at each of them, hoping for an answer, but they had none to give.

The three turned to Endril. "What did you dream?" Cal asked. He wondered if he would get an answer.

Endril paused. "It touched on a subject I have sworn to

keep secret. But I may tell you that Sillar spoke truly—my pride has been my bane. The dream spoke to me of the actions which sent me from my people, and the trials that were laid upon me. I dreamt that I had failed these tests, and stood before the great ones of my race, condemned and disgraced. All hope was abandoned, and I was in a place of despair and pain." He covered his face with his hands.

For a moment they were all silent. Then Bith said, "Let us leave this place. It is accursed!"

Endril looked up at her. "I cannot leave. I must find the sorceress, for I believe she can help defeat this evil, which is some new power of the Dark One. It is my duty—I must not ignore it. It was wrong of me to bring you here without your leave, but now I ask you: Will you travel with me, lady, gladly, and of your own choice?"

Bith gave him a gentle smile and nodded. "I will, my lord."

"And I," said Cal.

"And I," said Hathor.

"Thank you," Endril said simply.

"Well," Bith said, breaking a silence which was becoming awkward, "if you gentlemen will excuse me, I'll get ready."

"You look fine the way you are," Cal declared.

"Out." She looked as stern as she could and started pushing him from the room.

"I'm going, I'm going." He craned his head around. "Sure you don't need any help?"

She gave him a final shove and kicked the door shut after him. "Men!"

"Leaving, I see." John Sillar was seated on a pile of logs outside the inn. He was eating an apple. Bith eyed it greedily. She was starving.

"Here, take a few pippins." Sillar reached into his pack and pulled out handfuls of the tart apples. "Courtesy of Galen. You didn't seem to care much for his other food. With the money you gave him, he shouldn't begrudge you these."

He watched them as they devoured their breakfast. "And you're off to find the witch, eh? Well, I wish you good luck. Mayhap we'll meet again. And Sir Cal, thank you for the stories. By the time I'm done, you'll never be an unknown in these parts again."

"I'm not sure if I should be grateful or not," Cal whispered to Endril.

"Farewell, Master Sillar," Endril said. "If we meet again, we should have more tales for you." The four of them waved and then turned their horses to the road.

CHAPTER
3

As they rode farther from the village they saw that the countryside did change. The grass looked grey and withered. Trees were bare, stripped of their leaves.

Climbing higher into the mountains, they could see, from their vantage point, the desolation surrounding them. They met no one, and the few cottages they passed were deserted. The terraced fields were stripped and the barns and sheds empty. There was no sound save that of their horses' hooves. Even the birds seemed to have fled the place.

Cal halted, and fumbled in his pouch. He brought out a piece of paper, which he studied intently.

"What's that?" Bith asked.

"Some directions that Sillar wrote up last night, after you went to bed. It shows the best route to Mount Thalia. We should be near one of the landmarks he mentions."

"Stay by the side where there's the least brush, then turn right at the big rock that's mostly pink but looks a little grey if you're there early in the morning," Bith read. "Keep the ravine on your left. Go on riding until it's almost time for supper, and have an eye out for a boulder that looks like a face . . . . *This* is a route?"

"What did you expect, princess? Large signs saying 'This way to the sorceress?' We're lucky to have any information to guide us at all. This is pretty desolate country."

"Thank you for pointing that out. I would never have noticed on my own," Bith snapped back. "It must be all that military training that makes you so observant."

Cal didn't pay any attention to her. He was looking ahead at a large rock. "That reddish boulder may be what he meant."

Bith looked in the direction he was pointing. "I certainly hope you're right. I wouldn't like to get lost in this wasteland."

"Endril," Cal called. "I think we've found it."

They followed a rutted path up the mountain till they were alongside a large block of mottled stone. Looking downhill, they saw a ravine curving up and into the peaks.

"Now we're getting someplace," Cal said happily, and spurred his horse on.

"But where is someplace?" Bith asked the air. She didn't bother waiting for an answer.

The day seemed endless, and so did their journey. Soon, the sun was out but the air remained cold. Only a few clouds were in the sky, which arched over them in an endless sweep of space.

Toward the east, the land tilted up into a series of mesas, flat-topped and barren. To the west, the ground exploded into the air, forming the wall of mountains. Mount Thalia loomed ahead. In the silence and desolation they felt like they were the first persons on earth, or the last.

When the sun was high in the sky they stopped to eat. Endril and Cal had packed up some food from the night before. It tasted worse than ever, but they were so hungry they ate it anyway.

"Are we lost?" Hathor asked.

"We are on the right track, my friend," Endril replied.

"How will we know we have gotten to where we should be?" Hathor continued. His brow wrinkled. He wasn't sure what he had asked.

"That's a good question," Bith chimed in. "If we can't find the witch, how long do we wait to see if she'll find us?"

"We cannot stay long. We haven't the water nor the provisions, and it is really too cold to sleep outdoors," Endril answered. "Also, the land is too bare to provide decent forage for the horses." He cast his eyes about. "This place is indeed forbidding. I had not expected such desolation. It is unnatural. The farmers must have fled, and they have left nothing behind them."

Cal got up. "I'll go climb up those rocks and see what there is to see. Maybe I can spot something."

They watched him clamber up a slope and stare about him, his hand shading his eyes. He shouted, and beckoned for them to come over.

"Look, way over to the east . . . tell me what you see."

Endril, who had the clearest sight, said "I see something white and cloudy. It obscures my vision. I cannot see past it. I think it is the Mistwall."

They looked at each other. "I hope that sorceress shows up to help us," Cal said. "Things are going to come to a head here soon. Let's ride some more. We should try to find the next boulder before it gets dark."

At dusk, they came to the rock. Seen from the side, its jagged outline did look like a face, and a rather forbidding one at that. Near it stood a tumbledown hut. They dismounted and went inside and looked around. It was a very poor place—windowless and with a dirt floor. They noted a crude hearth and some kindling. No one was about, but from the onions and a loaf of brown bread that were set out on a rudely built table, they knew the place was inhabited.

"I'm sorry I complained about the inn last night," Bith said. "I should have known I'd be punished for it." She stooped to gather up some wood and start a fire. "Whoever lives here, I pity them."

"I hope *they* pity us," said Cal. "We've come here uninvited, and I'm thinking of gobbling down that loaf as soon as I warm up."

"We'll pay them," Bith said, shrugging. She held her hands out in front of the tiny blaze she'd started. "What I wouldn't give for a decent meal."

"It's too dark to hunt for anything," Cal replied. "And from the look of the land, I don't think I'd find so much as a lizard alive out there."

"Good," Bith answered. "I'm not that hungry. I said *decent* meal. Where's Endril?"

"He went to look for some water and take care of the horses. There must be some decent stream nearby if someone lives here. But I think he's also hoping this sorceress, or whatever she is, is going to creep up on him."

"Better him than us," Bith grumbled. "I still don't like this notion of looking up strange witches."

"Oh, hah, look what I found!" Hathor shouted. He was waving a small sack he'd spotted on the room's single shelf.

"What is it?" Cal asked. "Gold, jewels, roast pheasant?"

"Beans!"

Cal and Bith ran over to look. "Oooh," Bith said. "Let's make some stew."

"Oh, yes," Cal said with real fervor.

Endril came in, holding the dripping waterskins. "There's a small spring not far from here. We shan't die of thirst. And there's a bit of grass for the horses."

Bith snatched one of the skins from him. "You are mar-velous." Much to his surprise, she kissed him on the cheek. There was an iron pot by the hearth and she emptied the water into it, spilling some on the ground in her haste. Then she poured in the beans. "When it's almost cooked, we'll add the onions." She set the pot on the grate and stared at it impatiently. "I hope it'll be done soon."

Hathor joined her. "Ready in a little bit?"

"Ready in a big bit," Cal answered. "Beans take forever. Don't stare at it—you'll drive yourself mad. Here, eat some bread." He broke off chunks and handed them around.

Bith crammed a piece into her mouth. She looked at the rest of the loaf. "I suppose we should leave the rest," she said sadly. "If whoever lives here comes back, they won't be too pleased if we've left them nothing." She set the bread on the shelf so it wouldn't be so much of a temptation.

"Why don't you wave your wand or say a spell, princess, and conjure us up a feast?" Cal asked.

"I can't do that. It wouldn't be right."

"I think it sounds right."

Bith shook her head. "It would be like you using your sword to chop wood. You would never do that. It might damage the blade, and it would be a misuse of the weapon. Magic is much the same. It would be wrong to use magic for a trivial need that can be satisfied in some ordinary way. Casting a spell calls for courage and strength and concen-tration. Without these things, the spell may go away." Bith's voice took on a serious, thoughtful tone.

"My spells are not always successful, because I lack perfection in these qualities. The effect of a spell is the least important thing about it. It is nothing but the measure of the magician's strength of will and depth of understanding. Those are what really matter."

"I didn't want a lecture," Cal grumbled. "I just wanted

dinner. You're the one who said she was starving."

"Where did you learn these things?" Endril asked Bith. "Those are not your words."

Bith blushed. "I . . . I suppose from my mother. She often spoke of such matters."

Endril nodded, but made no comment.

Cal, of course, did. "If you learned it from Morea, all the more reason to distrust it. Why follow her teachings?"

"What do you know of my mother?" Bith demanded. Her silver eyes flashed. "Foolish boy, to speak slightingly of things you cannot understand! My mother may be many things, but inept she never was! Morea is a profound mistress of her art. As great as any of those heroes you keep on about."

Cal's mouth dropped open, but he had the sense, for once, to keep still.

"Dinner," Hathor said, placatingly. He banged a stick on the rim of the pot. "Come eat. I have apples left from the morning. Perhaps soon the stew will be done." Grateful for the interruption, they returned to their supper.

"I don't understand her," Cal complained to Endril. They were sitting in the doorway, looking out into the night. Bith was inside, wrapped in her cloak, staring into the fire. Hathor was already asleep.

"For months she's been talking about how evil Morea is, and how she's nothing like her. Then, when all I do is repeat something she's said a thousand times, she bites my head off. Women!"

Endril smiled. "It is a complicated matter."

"Women?"

Endril laughed. "Women—and everything else." He was quiet for a moment. "Let us be wary, Cal. This land seems peaceful . . . too peaceful. I feel uneasy. I think it best we keep a watch tonight. One of us on the alert, while the others sleep. What say you?''

"I think that is the wisest course. Shall I stand guard now?''

"No, you sleep. I feel restless.''

Cal went indoors. Bith, he saw, was asleep now, her face covered by her hair. She was breathing quietly and easily. Hathor was on his back, his mouth open, his arms flung wide. The sounds he was making were nothing worse than his usual night noises of snorts, an odd whistle or two, and snores. Perhaps their sleep would be free of evil dreams tonight. Cal made a place for himself against the wall closest to the fire, shut his eyes, and fell fast asleep.

Endril leaned against the doorpost, trying to make himself comfortable. He had always enjoyed being awake and alone at night. The world took on an added mystery and elusiveness that he welcomed. Too often, the hard-edged outlines revealed in bright daylight seemed constraints rather than indicators of the way things truly were. They were as deceptive, in their way, as the shadows that blurred and softened the world's face at night.

With his keen sight and hearing, he strained to catch any movement or sound that would betray another's presence. Surely he would hear the scrabble of tiny feet as animals came out to hunt for food, or the short, cutoff squeak of a mouse when it felt the owl's talons close around it? There was nothing.

As he listened to the silence he thought he sensed a tenseness about him, as if somewhere, beyond the immediate world of the senses, energies were being gathered in, collected for some final uncoiling that would shake the world like a bolt of lightning. It reminded him of the time before a summer thunderstorm.

Endril shook his head to clear it. These were fruitless

thoughts. Better to pay attention to any immediate dangers that might present themselves in the shape of a dagger's thrust or a spear's barbed tip. Better to listen and hope that the one he sought would appear, offering aid to him and his companions.

Endril shifted restlessly. This passivity irked him. He would much prefer seeking the witch out in her holdfast and making his demands known. He had always favored the role of leader to that of suppliant. This waiting for something to happen, or not, depending on the whim of another, was hard to bear.

Above, a shooting star flared briefly as it traveled across the sky—a brief, passionate spark of light in the autumn heaven. Behind him, he heard Bith call out in her sleep, then lapse again into silence. What dreams would come to her tonight? What dreams would come to them all?

Of all his companions, he thought Elizebith the oddest. Cal and Hathor he understood better. Their desires seemed straightforward, their characters as solid and true as a trusty staff or proven blade. But Bith was more difficult, a young woman filled with conflicting wants, and with a character that seemed a mixture of dark and light. She reminded him of himself, many years ago.

He had sometimes wondered who her father might be. Her mother had such a reputation for wantoness that trying to find the man might be impossible. Morea, herself, was a mystery. Bith did not know where she was, and the sorceress had made no effort to find her daughter.

Bith had spoken truly when she called her mother a mistress of her art. Morea was someone to be reckoned with, not a fairgrounds conjuror performing simple tricks for the gaping crowd's amusement. Endril thought that perhaps her thirst for knowledge had been an overriding one, driving her beyond the boundaries of caution and wisdom. Bith's statement that the effect of a spell was of little consequence was a curious one. What havoc had Morea wreaked, in her search for a more perfect understanding of her powers?

The lust for knowledge could be, he knew, as powerful as carnal desire. Such a passion could take many forms, and perhaps Morea's licentiousness was, finally, another manifestation of her uncontrolled need to know all—to penetrate every mask and disguise and know the secrets of another's being. And was she not the seduced as much as the seductress? The tempted as well as the temptress? Who could envy her, caught in the Dark One's snares, victim of her own desires?

Endril sighed. He felt he understood these traps very well, and was all too familiar with the haughty pride that had been the downfall of so many. Had not the elders . . .

He started. Surely, far in the distance, there had been a noise, the sound of pebbles dislodged, and whispers carried on the wind? Were not the shadows of night displaced and deformed by bodies moving through the dark emptiness that had surrounded them?

"Awake! I summon you!" a loud voice boomed in his ear. The door frame quivered. Endril leapt to his feet and whirled around, his dagger drawn.

Inside, the three sleepers stirred. They made the muffled, irritable sounds of people awakened abruptly from their slumbers.

"Enter, Endril. Your watch is vigilant, and your senses keen, but you must yield before the greater power of a lawful god." The voice was not only loud but smug.

Endril found his companions staring at the ground, into the puddle of water Bith had spilled earlier. When he too looked, he saw the bearded face of a man. He was richly dressed, in furs, and a gold chain hung about his neck. By some trick, the image was clear and undistorted. In the background was a many-turreted castle, gay with banners.

"Vili!" they said, their voices combined in a chorus of dismay.

"Yes, it is I, my faithful ones. You may do me homage, if you desire."

A deafening silence followed.

Vili raised his eyebrows. "No thanks, no gratitude for the fame and wealth I have bestowed on you? No worship for your greatest ally against the Dark One? I was warned that mortals are an ungrateful lot!"

"Ungrateful!" Bith screeched. "You've got your gall. Lord Vili, Ruler of the Twelve Spheres—hah!"

"In fact, it's Thirteen Spheres, my dear. I've advanced a bit since I saw you last. My powers are greater than before."

"That wouldn't take much," she said scornfully.

"What would you, Lord Vili?" Endril asked, his voice cold.

"Now, now, Endril. Don't get all stiff and formal with me. I know your elvish ways. You're simply piqued that I slipped in without you knowing it."

"Indeed, I am not. I was in no way lax in my duty. I was guarding the entrance, not pools of sludge. I am certain there is something moving about."

"Let us not quibble. It is undignified. Although, considering what I've done for you . . . ." He looked at Bith, whose mouth was open, ready to say something sarcastic. "That includes you, young lady. You've gotten more magical objects, and all of you have received gold, swords, fame . . . all sorts of things. However, I see no reason to quarrel." He beamed at them benevolently. "I bring you important news."

Hathor groaned.

"There is great danger," Vili said, in a voice fraught with gloom.

"What a surprise," said Bith.

Vili ignored her. "The Dark Lord is rising. To the east, the Mistwall encroaches."

Cal yawned.

"But perhaps you know this already?" There was disappointment in Vili's voice.

"Don't you think it odd that we're already here?" Cal asked. "What would we be doing in this forsaken place otherwise?"

"It surely isn't the accommodations," Bith said. She peered at the castle behind Vili. "You seem to be doing just fine, though." She scratched fiercely at her arm. "You know, I think there's fleas in this place."

Cal stared at her for a moment, and then took a very deliberate step backward. She snarled at him.

"Lord Vili," Endril said, "we thank you for this news. If you have nothing else to impart . . . "

"I do," Vili snapped. "The Dark Lord has acquired a new a weapon—an amulet of some sort. With it, he controls dreams and emotions. It is very likely his servant, Schlein, possesses the thing and is actually wielding it. He is still a novice, but his skill grows."

"We have some knowledge of this," Endril replied. "All of us have suffered foul dreams during our sleep."

"Then know this too . . . with this amulet a powerful sorcerer can give dreams and visions substance. Your worst terrors will no longer be penned up within the confines of sleep. They will walk abroad, as tangible to the senses as you are to each other." Vili could see, from their faces, that he had finally told them something new.

"I have other news," he continued. "I think you are all in more imminent danger. There are orcs prowling these mountains, advance spies of the Dark Lord's army. If they should catch . . . ''

There was a rush of air, and a spear rattled against the doorjamb. From outside, they heard high, squealing laughter.

''You see, I told you there was danger. I suggest you do something. There must be at least a dozen of them out there.''

''Quickly,'' Endril hissed. ''Against the wall.'' They pressed against the sides of the hut. ''Who goes there?'' Endril called out.

''Come out,'' replied a voice that sounded harsh and cruel. ''What manner of being are you who cowers in this hut? Show yourself, and perhaps we will kill you quickly. Trouble us, and we will kill you very, very slowly.'' There was more laughter.

''Come out, for we are hungry,'' called another voice.

''At least they don't know who we are,'' Endril said. ''That's something in our favor.''

''Why?'' Bith asked gloomily.

''Because they think there is only one of us, and they probably think it's some poor woodcutter or goatherd. They don't realize who they're dealing with,'' Cal said impatiently. ''The element of surprise is a tactical advantage.''

Hathor swung his axe in a powerful arc. ''We see who eats,'' he growled. ''I surprise them.''

''We need a plan,'' Endril said. His bow was in his hand. Another spear flew into the hut. ''Cal, you . . . ''

But there was no time. Caltus Talienson, the hero of Cairngorm, had run out into the night with drawn sword, screaming for blood.

CHAPTER
4

Endril shouted in exasperation, "The fool! What's he trying to prove? After him! Bith, stay to the rear. Hathor, you come with me." They could hear screams and yells. The three rushed outdoors.

Cal was surrounded, orcs all around him. His sword flashed in the starlight. He was shouting strange words no one could understand, and on his face was a look of rapture. He was transported beyond fear. The orcs fell back before him, their red eyes wide in the blackness. Each time the glittering sword bit home there were squealing sounds, and a pair of red eyes would shut.

The sight of blood increased his frenzy, and Cal hacked his way through his enemies. He was as bold and merciless as a thunderstorm in the mountains. Before him, he saw creatures kneeling—whether in supplication or death, it mattered not. Their passing was of no importance. There was a screaming in his ears but it sounded sweet, like music. It was homage, praise of his greatness.

Endril watched him, and for all his peril, he gaped. The boy was possessed, it was clear. But by what? Had Vili inhabited his body, filling him with the fury of a war god?

Then there was a blow, and Endril fell to the ground, borne down by an orc. They grappled on the cold earth. Endril felt brutal hands pinning him to the ground, and a foul, acrid smell filled his nostrils. The orc grinned, revealing sharp yellow fangs. He bent low, ready to bite out his captive's throat.

Desperately, Endril bucked, arching his back and bringing up his knees. The orc lost his balance for a moment, but for a moment only. The viselike grip tightened again, and he gave a howl of triumph. He stooped toward his victim, then toppled over and stared blankly up into the night. His skull had been riven in two.

Hathor pulled Endril to his feet. "My friend," the elf gasped, "I owe you my life. I thought those fangs would be the last sight I would ever see."

Hathor shrugged. "Was no trouble, but not wise to daydream here." Without a backward glance, he marched back into the fray, swinging his heavy axe with the deliberation of a man chopping wood.

"Let's work our way to Cal," Endril said. He was walking back to back with the troll, covering him from the rear. Hathor grunted and glanced in the boy's direction. "We need help more—he should come here."

"He seems a bit preoccupied," Endril gasped, as he shot an arrow into an oncoming orc. This time Hathor was too busy to answer. He was fighting desperately with a tall, strongly built orc, whose body was covered in chain mail and whose face was hidden by his helmet. He wielded a huge broadsword, and as the axe and sword struck each other, sparks went shooting into the night.

With a powerful stroke, the orc sent the axe spinning from Hathor's hands. Hathor gaped in surprise. To the troll, everything seemed to slow down after that. He saw the broadsword rise again and gracefully lift up over the orc's shoulder. It moved as gently and lightly as milkweed on a breezy spring day. There it hovered, glittering, for long moments before it began its slow descent.

Hathor stared at the bright blade, mesmerized. He heard Endril shout something, and he started forward. He ducked under the orc's guard and wrapped his arms around his waist. Time speeded up. Hathor gave a bloodcurdling yell and picked the orc up and hurled him away, like someone tossing a heavy boulder.

"Well done, my friend," Endril called. "Soon we shall be hearing songs about you, as well as Cal."

"Songs are very dull," Hathor replied. "Trolls do not sing. After a battle, there is a great feast." He licked his lips. Endril decided not to ask him what it was that trolls feasted on.

"Cannot find axe," Hathor complained. He began ripping up huge chunks of earth and heaving them at his enemies. He was snarling. "Axe been in family many years."

An arrow, its barb aflame, flew by them and landed in the hut's thatched roof. Soon, there was the smell of smoke, as fire embraced the house. The air around it shimmered with the heat.

"Bith, where are you?" Endril shouted. There was no answer.

From atop a hill, Bith gazed down at the battle. She had no skill with blade or bow, and knew she would be useless in armed combat. Better to stay clear than be an added trial to her companions. Also, she had weapons of her own, and did not need to grapple with her enemies face to face.

From the pouch at her belt Bith pulled out her wand. The silver object gleamed as brightly as any blade. She had rarely used it, and admitted to herself that she did not understand its properties. But she suspected it would make any spell she recited more powerful, and power was what she wanted now.

Bith knelt on the ground and picked up a small, sharp rock. Tension built inside her. Did the wand glow more brightly? She wasn't sure. "Courage and strength of will, Elizebith," she told herself. "Do not waver. Now is not the time for faintheartedness." Quietly she intoned:

> Let the spirits of earth heed me.
> I give blood for dominion over thee.
> Let my desires be thine,
> Break thy confines,
> Appear, spirit, I charge thee.

She took the rock and slashed it across her palm. The long, shallow cut filled with blood and channeled it like a gutter. Bith watched as the blood dripped off her hand and splashed to the earth. She felt dizzy, but steeled herself.

Now she was sure the wand had grown brighter.

"What wouldst thou?" a voice whispered from somewhere behind her. It sounded dark and clotted, the voice of something that dwelt in a dark cavern underground. At her back, Bith felt a presence, a pressure bearing against her. She did not turn around. "I demand thy obedience, spirit. Do as I say."

"Thy voice is firm, but thy will shakes. Thou art but a babe in these matters. Who are you to command me? I shall drag thee beneath the earth and there torment thee for thy insolence. Thou shalt be my captive and slave for as long as these mountains stand." The pressure against her increased.

"I am one who knows full well what she may and may not do, lackwit," Bith answered. "I called thee, knowing completely what I was about. Thou art a paltry thing. Obey me, or suffer my wrath. Threaten me, and thou shalt pay. I have no time to trifle.'' Without quite knowing why, Bith struck the wand sharply against the rock. The voice gave forth a high, mewling sound.

''We merely asked, great sorceress. There is no need for fury.'' Now the voice seemed conciliatory, almost cringing. ''What do you wish, queenly mistress?''

''Spare me your flattery, liar,'' Bith said coldly. ''I know thee and all thy ways. Your mind lies plain before me.'' She paused, gathering her strength. There must be no uncertainty in her voice. ''I would have you destroy the enemy below. Let the boulders of this mountain crush them.''

''Is that your only wish, lady?''

''I have no wishes—only fulfilled desires. Between the wish and the doing there shall be no difference.''

There was a tittering laugh. ''But you ask so little. Would you not like the very mountain to crumble, or domain over my army of lesser spirits? I can bestow great power. But give me your bond, and you shall walk down this mountain a goddess. All shall fear you. You will be as beautiful and terrible as a comet in the sky.''

Bith laughed, but it was a laugh filled with scorn. There was no mirth in it. Again, she struck the wand, and again came the sound of pain.

''I warned thee, liar. I warned thee, false tempter. Think you that I do not know what you are—a worm, a spirit considered lowly even among the lowliest? Thy blandishments are useless. If ever I make such a pact, it will be for more than empty words. Thou hast my blood and my strength. Do my bidding, or suffer more pain.'' She raised the wand again.

''No, no, lady. I will do as you command.'' The voice seemed to change again, and become more menacing. ''Someday, you must choose. I will wait for that day. I know your name, Elizebith, daughter of Morea.''

The sense of a presence vanished. Bith was alone. She fell forward and lay on the ground, exhausted. All in all, however, she was pleased with her performance. She had conjured only a very minor spirit, knowing she could hope to control no more, and that for but a short space of time. And, really, it was all that was necessary. She had escaped the encounter unscathed. A tone of sarcasm and haughtiness always worked well with these creatures. They were mostly empty brag and boast. Still, she wished it hadn't called her by name. It was unsettling. Now, though, the question was, Would the thing do her bidding?

Bith felt the ground tremble beneath her. She scrambled to her feet. *It worked!* she thought. *How about that!* Then another thought came to her: *I have to warn the others! We've got to get out of here.* She began running down the hill.

Endril heard a roar, and amidst the roar was a voice that seemed to be calling his name. There was a pause in the fight. Swords hung in midair, heads turned, eyes widened, mouths dropped open. Someone was running downhill, shouting, leading an army of boulders. The orcs turned and fled. Cal, cheated of his prey, chased after them, screaming for vengeance. He looked like a madman.

Endril saw that the running figure was Bith. "Get out of the way," she called. "You'll be crushed." Endril and Hathor took a wild dive out of the path of the oncoming rocks. Bith followed them. The stones clattered down the hillside and rolled about the ground, crashing into each other and knocking each other about. Finally, they came to rest.

Hathor slowly got to his feet. "Endril, Bith, where are you?" There was a sound like sliding gravel, and the two of them emerged from behind a clump of brush. Both were dusty and they were coughing a little.

"Very effective, Bith," Endril managed to say.

"Thank you," she gasped.

"Perhaps, next time, you could give us some warning?"

"Really, I don't see how I had the opportunity."

Endril sighed. "I suppose you're right." He slapped his clothes, raising clouds of dust. Bith sneezed.

"Pardon me, Bith"

"It's quite all right." She sneezed again.

Hathor was standing in the ruins of the burnt hut, kicking through the rubble.

"What have we lost, Hathor?" Endril asked.

The troll shrugged. "Little. Is good we sleep in clothes."

"Speak for yourself," Bith muttered.

"Rest of bread all burnt, stew burnt," Hathor said unhappily. "We have little left to . . . "

"There's Cal!" Bith shouted. "What's wrong with him?"

Cal was standing amid the rocks, shouting and swinging his sword. But his movements weren't wild and unplanned. Instead, he seemed to be battling an invisible foe, for his sword strokes were deliberate, and his eyes were fixed on a particular place in the air, as if he were looking in someone's eyes.

Cautiously, they approached him. Endril motioned for everyone to keep still.

"Coward!" Cal cried. "You won't escape this time. No one can call me craven. You'll pay for that lie with your life."

He lunged forward, a savage expression on his face. The sword whistled through the air.

He laughed. "You are nimble. It will not save you. I shall keep after you until I have your head. You will never escape me.'' He jumped back, as if to avoid the cut of a sword. Then he leaped forward again. "Death!" he screamed. He stabbed into the air with his sword and shouted in triumph. "Who shall be next? I will have vengeance."

"What's going on here?" Bith whispered to Endril. "Is he mad?"

Endril shook his head, then said something quietly in Hathor's ear. The troll nodded.

"Caltus Talienson," Endril called out. "Brave warrior, do you know me?" He began walking forward very slowly, with his hands in plain sight. Cal turned and stared at Endril. "I do not. Where is your flag? With whom do you fight?"

"With you, as always," Endril answered. "We have been companions-at-arms many times. Can you not recall?"

"Your face, I have seen it," Cal said hesitantly. "But as if in a dream." His voice hardened. "You are a sorcerer. You have bewitched my men, and Sir Edric. I know you now, deceiver! Prepare yourself, for I fear you not!"

He leapt toward Endril, who dodged quickly and ran toward Hathor. His foot caught on one of the rocks and he fell forward. Cal was on him in an instant, and Bith screamed. Hathor, moving with surprising speed, knocked Cal flat with a single blow to the jaw. Cal moaned once, then lay still.

They rushed over to him. "I think you've killed him, Hathor," Endril said, stooping over the boy.

"No, no, he be fine . . . just be eating porridge for a bit."

"He's breathing," Bith announced. "He's going to have a fine bruise on that jaw, though."

Endril peered into Cal's face. "What do you suppose all that was about? He didn't even recognize us."

"Magic, I think," Hathor said. "He was bewitched."

"It was either magic or drink," said Bith. "And if it was drink, I want to know where he got it."

Once he knew Cal was fine, Hathor seemed to lose interest. He began roaming about, moving rocks from his path, and staring fixedly at the ground. "Aha," he called. He had found his axe. He waved it over his head. "Let us leave this place now," he said. "We cannot stay. No food. Strange dangers. It is a bad place."

"Alas, my wise friend," Endril said, "you are right. I had never thought we would find the land so bare and deserted, its people so hostile, and the Dark Lord's minions creeping about. As you say, we must leave. Our quest for the sorceress is over before it has fairly begun. I planned this venture very poorly." His shoulders sagged.

Neither Bith nor Hathor, on the other hand, looked particularly dismayed. "Where are saddles and bridles and horses?" Hathor asked.

Endril clapped his hand to his head. "The horses! Bith, come with me. Hathor, stay with Cal. There's no telling what he'll be like when he awakens." He ran off toward the stream he had found, and Bith trailed after him. The horses were still there, cropping the meager grass that grew by the stream. They pricked up their ears when they saw them coming, and trotted over. Plainly, they were hoping someone was going to feed them.

Endril spotted the saddles and bridles sitting on the rocks where he had left them the night before. "Alas, my friends," he said to the horses. "I'm afraid you must suffer with the rest of us. Food is scarce." He rummaged in his saddlebag and brought out some more apples. He sliced them and fed the horses. They seemed to like the apples, and began nuzzling him, trying to find more.

"As little as I look forward to it, I must save the rest for ourselves."

"They can have my share," Bith said.

"No, you'll need to eat them. If we ride hard all day we

can make the village where we breakfasted yesterday, but there will be little to sustain us on the way.''

They started saddling the horses. As he was tightening a girth Endril asked, ''How did you cause that rockslide?''

Bith shrugged. ''It was easy. I summoned a spirit—a very minor one, of course.''

''And what price did you pay?''

Bith showed him her cut hand. ''It was nothing. The wand helped. It gives me more power to control them. Afterward, I was tired, but it worked.'' Her eyes sparkled. ''I have never managed to control an elemental, before. My skill grows.''

Endril nodded, but said nothing.

''You seem displeased. Why?''

''I am not displeased, Elizebith. I simply fear for you. What you did had great risk in it.''

''And what you and Cal and Hathor did—was that too not dangerous? Why should my risks be any the less? Just as Cal wishes to attain great prowess with his blade, so do I wish for great skill in my art. He does not run from danger. None of you do. Neither shall I.'' She sounded proud and defiant.

Endril bowed to her.

''We're done here,'' Bith said. ''Let's get back. Cal may come to at any time. Are the waterskins filled?''

''Indeed. We are ready to journey back.''

''Good. I've had enough of this place.'' They led the horses to where Hathor stood. Cal hadn't moved.

Bith peered down at him, a small smile on her lips. ''Poor lad,'' she murmured. ''He should be awakened with a kiss.'' She took one of the waterskins that hung from her saddle's pommel, and unceremoniously emptied it onto Cal.

He sat up abruptly, choking and spluttering. Hathor

started to laugh. Endril looked irritated. "Your methods, Elizebith . . . "

Bith shrugged. "How are you feeling, Cal? Refreshed from your little nap?"

"What!" Cal said, shaking his head to get the water from his eyes. "What's . . . why am I on the ground?" He glared up at Bith. "I'll get you for this."

"I was just trying to help," Bith said, giving him her sweetest smile.

"No doubt," he muttered. He tried to stand and almost lost his balance. Hathor and Endril steadied him. "You'll be fine in a moment, lad," Endril said.

"I can stand . . . I can stand. Let me be for a moment." Reluctantly, they let go, keeping near in case he fell again. But, this time, Cal stood on his own.

He rubbed his jaw. "Who hit me?" he demanded. "An orc?"

Hathor blushed. "Me."

Cal gaped at him.

"Don't you remember anything?" Bith asked. "You almost killed Endril."

"You're insane," Cal retorted, his eyes wide.

Endril stepped between them. "What *do* you remember?"

Cal paused to gather his thoughts. "We were in the hut, and Vili was telling us things we already knew. Then we were attacked. I felt . . . " He paused, groping for words. "I felt something inside me. It was as though I were the outer shell but there was an inner being controlling me. And that being was not myself. I think it was Vili."

"It is as I suspected," Endril said. "His powers grow."

"Now I'm angry about it," Cal continued. "He had no right to do that. But while it was happening, it was wonderful. I felt like I had drunk some heady wine, and I was beyond anything so petty as fear.

"I no longer felt human. None of you mattered to me anymore. I was simply an instrument of wrath, doling out punishment to those who had troubled me. I wasn't defending you, or helping you, or even helping myself. There were no distractions, because I knew I was invulnerable. There would have been no appeal for any creature that got in my way." He shivered. "It's frightening in a way, but it was glorious while it lasted.

"Then there was that landslide . . . your doing, I suppose?" He looked at Bith, who curtseyed in response. "I thought so," Cal said.

"After the orcs ran away, I felt emptied out. Something had left me. But it wasn't over yet. I found myself in battle again, but it was the place where I fought with Sir Edric and everyone thought we ran away."

He flushed a bit. "I've often thought about that day, and the shame it brought upon us. Many a time I've wished I could relive it, and avenge myself on those who played us for such fools. And that's exactly what I thought was happening. I didn't even stop to question it. I don't know why."

He looked at his friends. "What was I doing?"

"Murdering the air," Endril said. "There was nothing there."

"It was so real," Cal murmured. "It even smelled the same. The air was heavy with the scent of lilacs that day. Lilacs and death. I can never forget it.

"I must have thought you were one of the enemy," he said to Endril.

"You accused me of being the sorcerer who had bewitched Sir Edric and yourself. You were quite determined to kill me."

"Thank you for stopping me," Cal said to Hathor. He

grinned and then winced. "You've a powerful arm."

Hathor grinned in turn. "Oh, yes, trolls are very strong. Good wrestlers, good fighters."

"Do you feel steady enough to ride, Cal?" Endril asked.

"Of course! I'm fine. What kind of a warrior can't survive a sore jaw?"

"You are a fierce warrior, and no mistake," Endril said, smiling. "I can witness to that. I thought I'd be skewered for sure."

"Where are we off to? Further up the mountain?"

"No. The quest is done. We have neither food nor shelter, and we can't risk another encounter like the one last night. We'll journey back, telling folk of their danger, along the way. Let us reach town, and there decide what our next move should be."

"Suits me. Town life has more and more to say for it as rations and daylight grow short."

"Look!" said Hathor.

"What now?" Bith asked.

An old woman was approaching, climbing slowly up the mountain trail. She was humpbacked and dirty. Her clothes were tattered brown rags that fluttered about her in the light wind. Stringy grey hair obscured her face. She was leaning on a gnarled stick that served for a cane. Strapped to her back were branches and clumps of brush. She was weeping.

Cal came up to her. She smelled sour, he thought. Like a room that had been shut up for a long time. He had been in poorly kept stables that smelled much the same. "What ails you, mother?"

"Oh, sir," she answered, in a thin, quavering voice, "I seen monsters, and now, my home . . . " Overcome, she pointed toward the smoking rubble of the hut.

Cal gingerly touched her shoulder. "We will help you. We stayed in your cottage last night, before the monsters you spoke of destroyed it. We owe you for a night's lodging and food. Tell us what you have seen."

"I do not know. There were many black things, shaped like my old kettle, if my kettle had legs. Terrible fierce they were, with red eyes and claws. They were running over the mountain like an army of ants. I hid till they passed me by, then hied myself home, but it is no more. What has happened? What will become of me?" Her voice rose higher, becoming a keening wail of misery.

Hathor came up to her and offered her an apple, but she refused. "I thank you for your kindness," she said through her tears, "but, as you can see, I can't eat the raw stuff no more." She opened her mouth wide, revealing a few crooked brown stumps and nothing else. Bith averted her eyes. "If I can't gum it," the old woman continued, "or cook it, I can't eat it. And now I've no hearth as well as no teeth."

She hobbled over to what was left of the hut and started poking through the ashes with her stick. "Gone, gone," she wailed.

Bith watched her with narrowed eyes. "What's your name, old woman?" she demanded in a harsh voice.

"Meg, my lady." The woman touched her forehead respectfully. "Old Meg, they call me. I make brooms and sell bits of kindling."

"Be gentle with her, Bith," Cal whispered. "She's had a bad time."

"Maybe," Bith answered, glaring at the woman. "If she's what she seems. I'm not so sure. Besides, I can't abide wretchedness. She should be glad the filthy place is gone. How can anyone stand such destitution? Her spirit should have rebelled against it long ago!"

"Her life is the life of many," Endril said. He eyed the

woman. "How long have you dwelt in these parts, Old Meg?"

"Oh, many years, sir. First me and my man; then, when he died, by myself. You can ask about me in the village below. They know Old Meg and I know them."

"What were you doing, wandering about all night?" Bith demanded.

"Oh, mistress, when you reach my age, you'll find you no longer sleep easily. A long night's rest is the privilege of the young. The old are more wakeful. Often I wander these hills for days, sheltering in caves, gathering what I need to make my brooms and sell my kindling. I know these mountains better than almost anyone. And lately, I've had to wander farther and farther afield to find what I need. This is not such a friendly place as it once was." She sighed. "We're coming to a bad end, all of us. That's the only thing that's certain."

"Have you heard anything of a sorceress who haunts these parts?" Endril asked.

The old woman cackled. "Aye, I know of her. I know what no other mortal does—where she hides herself, away from the prying sight of folk like us. There, the air is not as it is here, for the trees bear fruit, and the grass is still green."

Endril's eyes lit up. "You have been to this place?"

"I have seen it with my own eyes, but only from afar. I wouldn't dare to venture close. She's a tricky one, they say. What if she turned me into a toad, or suchlike?" Meg hobbled over to Endril and grasped his arm.

"I'll tell you how I found it. One day I spied a little path what led further up than is my habit to go. I says to myself, 'Meg, you've scoured the old ways clean. It's time to try another way.' So up I go, and with these poor legs of mine, it was no mean feat, let me tell you! Soon the path gives out and there's nothing but rock, but I'm a stubborn one, I am." She cackled. "My old man used to say I was stubborn as an old mule. He'd hit me with the broom, so angry he'd get." She paused a moment and then went on.

"Through a terrible windy pass, and then down for a bit, then up again goes I. I come to a place that looks out over a valley." Her voice became hushed. "And there, in that valley, everything is green and fresh, but queer somehow. I could never really see it, if you take my meaning. It was like trying to look at something through your own tears, or out of the corner of your eye. You never really had it clear before you. I knew I'd either gone mad or it was a bewitchment. I left, so scared I was. But I've gone back a few times since. It was too beautiful to let alone—like a place you'd dream about." She sighed. "It's worth the climb. Now, you tell me: Who else could work such a marvel but the sorceress herself?"

"Will you take us to that place?" Endril asked.

"Oh, sir, I don't know. . . . "

"We'll pay you," Bith broke in.

The woman's eyes lit up. "I could use a bit of money, and that's the truth, my lady. It's been hard times for me lately, and harder to come." She gestured toward the ruins of the house.

Endril pulled a gold coin from his pouch. The woman snatched at it, but he pulled it away. "Show us this valley, and it's yours. Is the path leading down to it plain from this overlook you mention?"

"Oh, yes, sir," Meg replied. Her eyes were fixed on the coin. "It's not a bad scramble down, as these things go." She turned her eyes back to Endril. "But I won't enter it with you. I want nothing to do with sorcery."

"Done," Endril answered. "But show us how to get down, and if all is as you say, you'll be well paid."

"And no tricks," Bith broke in. "I tell you now, old woman, that I too am a sorceress." Meg backed away, her eyes wide.

"You do well to fear," Bith continued. Her voice was cold and haughty, her face scornful. "I am here to challenge this so-called sorceress. Next to me, she is but a charlatan. And any old fool who thinks she can cheat me . . ." Bith left the sentence uncompleted and glared meaningfully at Meg, who cowered before her.

"Let this be a slight demonstration of my power," Bith said, pulling out her wand. She shut her eyes and recited:

> A ring of fire—
> A band of light
> To burn the liar
> And blast her sight.
> False one beware,
> Traitor take care,
> Break not thy trust,
> Or die thou must.

Bith waved her wand around Meg and, for a brief moment, a ring of flame encircled the old woman's feet—a flame that gave off no heat. Meg shrieked, "Mercy, mercy, don't kill me, mistress!" The flames flickered and died.

"Remember," Bith told her. "Remember well what I can do when I choose."

Meg bowed to her repeatedly. "I will be faithful, my lady, I promise you. Truly, you are a great sorceress. I have never seen such power."

"It's all right," Cal said. "She won't harm you. Lead us to this place. All will be well."

• • •

They began to climb, matching themselves to Meg's slow pace. Cal drew next to Bith. "Was that little display of yours necessary?"

Bith shrugged. "Maybe. I don't see why we should trust this woman because we pity her. We don't know anything about her. I wouldn't have hurt her, really."

"She could have died of fright. I think you were too harsh."

"Think what you like. Who's to say she won't lead us to a deep crevasse? She knows we have money and horses. What sort of temptation must they be to her? I have been poor and hungry, and, when I was, my morals were none too nice. And I had suffered for only a short while. What of this one, who has been hungry most of her life?"

Cal looked at her for a long moment, and shook his head. "You never cease to puzzle me, princess. You are the oddest mix of sweetness and hardness I have ever seen." He decided to change the subject. "Where did you learn that little trick with the fire?"

"Oh, that. I learned it as a young child. It's little more than a nursery rhyme. Young apprentices do it when they've drunk too deeply of their master's ale. A trick, as you say, and little more."

Cal snorted. "That's what you were taught as a child? What about jacks, or hoops, or dollies?"

"And when you were a child, my guess is you ran about with a wooden sword and shield and slew imaginary dragons," Bith retorted. "And your parents stood by and laughed and urged you on. Is it not so?"

"That was different!"

"How so? Although you were too young to know, you were being trained for the path that had been chosen for you. It was the same for me. Both of us were set upon our roads before we fairly knew what we were about."

"Perhaps what you say is true," Cal admitted. "But I am content with my road. Can you say the same?"

Bith laughed. "By the time I decide that, I shall be as old as that crone who leads us." She looked at the straggling line Hathor, Endril, and Meg made ahead of her. "Hey there," she shouted. "Can't we go any faster? If we must go to this place, then let's get there!"

It was not an easy road. The old woman, who was surprisingly nimble, had first led them up a rocky trail that seemed fit for nothing but mountain goats. Then the trail had died away into nothing, and there was only rock and scrub to mark their way. The horses picked their way cautiously over the rubble and balked at the crevices lining the route.

As they climbed higher, they began gasping and had to rest more and more often. Only Meg was unaffected. As they moved toward the mountain's crown, her step became more elastic, her pace quicker. Even Endril could not keep up with her.

"Truly, mother, you shame me," Cal wheezed, at one of their frequent rest stops. "I thought myself a hardy man, but you beat me hollow."

Meg cackled. "The mountains are my life's blood. Abide up here awhile, young master, and you'll best any mere lowland warrior without half trying. There's nothing like clean, thin air to make you hale as an ox."

"I have no wish to be an ox," Bith said sulkily.

"Oh, but mistress, you have your great magical powers to rely on. We poor folk have only our muscles."

Bith eyed her suspiciously. Was the old hag mocking her?

Hathor said, "I strong as ox, but even the ox need air. How much more?"

"Soon, my long-fanged friend." Meg pointed to another upward stretch of barren rock. "Up that final hill, and you shall see a great wonder."

"Hill!" Cal craned his neck. "You call that a hill?"

Endril rose slowly to his feet. "I too am weary, my friends, but let us continue. We are so close."

Their pace slowed to a painful trudge, with Meg far in the lead. Bith could hear the blood pounding in her ears, and she had to stop every few feet, doubled over, gasping for breath. In the thin air, the sun beat down mercilessly and the sweat trickled down her back. Her companions were faring as badly.

Meg had reached the summit. She was shouting and pointing at something. "Here, masters; here, mistress, come and see! Look how lovely. Hurry!"

Spurred by her words, they scrambled up the rest of the slope. They stared out onto the land. Below them, sunk deep among the grim peaks, was a valley, green and pure, glittering in the sun.

CHAPTER
5

They gasped in amazement. The tiny island of green, nestled in a sea of grey rock, looked like an exquisite miniature carved of jade. But it was as old Meg had told them. In the thin air they saw it with an unreal clarity; yet the details eluded them. The magical land seemed to waver and shimmer, like a coy illusion. If they turned away for a moment, they could not recall exactly what they had seen. The memory had no more permanence than the half-remembered fragment of a dream.

"Is too pretty," Hathor said. "Hurts the eyes."

"We must get down there," Endril muttered. His face was eager, impatient.

"I've kept my word, master," Old Meg reminded him. "Is it not exactly as I've said?"

"It is, indeed," Endril murmured.

"There's your best path, master." Meg pointed downward. "Stay to the right of that big crevice, and follow the slope where the larger boulders lie. That should bring you and yours safely down."

"It is all as you have promised, Meg." Endril pulled two

gold coins from his pouch and pressed them into the woman's hand.

Meg stared at them. "Oh, thank you, sir. 'Tis a sight more wondrous than any valley. Copper has been my lot for most of my life, and a few times silver. Gold is something I've never seen." She curtseyed to all four of them. "Good luck to you all. And, mistress," she said, turning to Bith, "I know you will triumph and claim all this for your own. Who could stand against someone like you?"

Meg bowed again and began clambering down the mountainside. "I don't think I trust that woman," Bith muttered. "And I know I don't like her."

Endril was already scrambling down the slope. The others hesitated, unsure of whether they wanted to follow or not. "What's the matter?" the elf called back.

"Is strange place," Hathor said uneasily.

"I'm going ahead," Endril replied. "Do what you will." He turned his back on them and continued on his way. Bith, Hathor, and Cal looked at each other briefly, and then followed him. "We're going to regret this," Bith said.

They walked for the better part of the afternoon. The ground looked too treacherous for riding, so they walked footsore and weary, toward the valley, which never seemed to grow closer. Their horses pranced about, their ears pricked, their eyes wide, and Endril wondered what it was that they were noticing. Though all his senses strained for some sound or sign, he could detect nothing.

"Perhaps it is only an illusion," Cal finally suggested. He was feeling tired and out of sorts. "We have been haunted by dreams and phantoms. Remember, too, what Vili said. This could be a delusion, conjured up by Schlein. Maybe we should turn back, before we find ourselves in a dungeon or worse."

"I do not think so," Endril answered. "Those other dreams brought fear and unhappiness. I feel neither. Do any of you quake before the sight of this valley?"

His three companions shook their heads. "I feel something," Bith said, sounding puzzled. "But I'm not sure what. There is a presence, and as we draw closer, it seems stronger. This is no illusion."

"I agree with Bith," Endril said. "What say you, Hathor?"

The troll snuffled loudly. He was taking in the air in great gulps. "Apples," he announced. "I smell apples."

"That's our saddlebags," Cal said. "They stink from the fruit we got at Galen's inn."

"No," Hathor said. He sounded very definite. "These are fresh, not been lying in some old cellar for months."

Endril stopped in his tracks. He too sniffed the air. "Hathor is right. I smell sweet air, and fruit trees. Let us hurry."

As the afternoon lengthened into evening, the ground leveled off, and at last they saw a path. Not the barely visible, rocky trails they had been scrambling over for the past two days, but a path that was wide, flat, and flagged with grey stone. Trees, their leaves deeply colored with the reds and golds of autumn, lined the walkway. The smell of ripe fruit was heavy in the air.

A sense of peace and well-being surrounded them. Birds were flying about overhead, and crickets were chirping in the grass. A gentle breeze had sprung up, drying the sweat from their bodies.

"This is too good to be true," Bith said. "All it lacks is a rainbow and some lambs leaping about."

"Is pretty," Hathor said. "I like it here."

"You would," Bith retorted. "How can you be so trusting?"

Hathor looked at her in surprise. "Why should I not trust? Much is good, much is nice." He reached up and plucked a pear from a tree. It smelled like nectar. He bit into it with relish, letting the juice run down his chin. "Is tasty. Should try one." He picked another and gave it to Bith. "Eat," he urged her. "Is not evil, is not poison."

She nibbled at the pear. "Not bad," she admitted grudgingly. She took a bigger bite of the sweet flesh. Endril and Cal also took some pears. They ate hungrily, devouring them in a few gulps.

"I wonder if there's anything else to eat around here?" Cal said. "Maybe we should try to find a house. It will be dark soon."

"Let us follow this path to its end," Endril replied. "This place has been so good to us, I am sure we will find food and lodging."

As they continued on their way, they saw more signs that the land was inhabited. They passed a garden, ripe and heavy with its harvest. Squash and pumpkins lay on the ground, and tall rows of corn waved gently in the breeze. Herbs, neatly growing among the rows of vegetables, flavored the air with their sweet smells. Hathor's mouth was watering.

Beyond, they saw a barn, where they stabled their horses. Next to it was a hen roost. "Chickens," Cal breathed. "Just think . . . chicken pie, with gravy and onions, and a nice brown crust." He held his stomach and groaned. "No carrots, though," he added thoughtfully. "I can't abide carrots—especially when they're cooked. Too mushy."

"I'll be sure and tell the chef," Bith said. "Does anyone else have any requests before I send in the menu for this evening's collation?"

"I'd like rabbit, milady," Endril said, joining in the game. "Rabbit cooked in wine, onions, and herbs, and covered with a buttermilk crust. I'd also like a fresh salad.''

"Duly noted. And you, Hathor, your tastes are so simple. Is there nothing more fanciful than your usual fare that would tempt your palate?''

"Strawberries," Hathor said immediately. His rather crudely wrought face took on the dreamiest expression Bith had ever seen. "With cream, lots and lots of thick cream.''

"I shall see to it, sir." Bith dropped a graceful curtsey.

"And you, princess, what would you like?" Cal asked.

Bith answered without any hesitation. "A hot bath."

The walkway led them straight to a house. It wasn't large, but it looked comfortable. It was faced with grey stone and the windows were covered with blue shutters. They went up to the door and knocked. No one answered.

"Should we go in?" asked Cal.

"Why not?" Bith answered. "We never hesitated going into that disgusting hovel last night. I see no reason to stand on ceremony simply because this place has proper walls and a door. Waiting to be invited into someone's home simply isn't done anymore." She opened the door and walked in. Her friends looked at each other, shrugged, and followed her.

Inside, there was a fire blazing in the hearth. The room felt warm and comfortable. Tapestries of hunting scenes covered the walls. A winding staircase led to the upstairs rooms. "Hello?" Endril called. "Is anyone here?" he shouted up the stairwell. There was no answer.

"Someone must be at home," Cal said. "No one just leaves a house like this unattended, with a fire blazing and the door open."

"But this is not just a house," Endril answered. "We are in an enchanted valley, in the home of a sorceress. She may not choose to do as others would."

Hathor was wandering around the room, examining the

tapestries and trying out all the chairs. "Very comfortable," he said approvingly, as he plopped down into one. He sighed happily and stretched out his legs in front of the fire. "Let's live here," he suggested.

"Right," Cal said. "Bith, you told Meg you were going to challenge the sorceress for her holding. We may just make you carry out that threat." Bith ignored him.

"We must not forget what we are here to accomplish," Endril said. "Comfort is all very well, but we are here to get aid for our cause." Everyone ignored Endril.

Cal went into one of the adjoining rooms and found, to his great delight, that it was the dining room, and the table was laden with covered dishes.

"Food," he shouted. Everyone ran in.

"Let's eat," he urged, sitting down at the table.

Bith gaped. "Look," she said, as she lifted the covers from the dishes. "Rabbit pie, chicken pie, vegetable stew, greens, and a rack of lamb. Very funny. I knew there would be lambs in it someplace. We're being spied on."

"No strawberries?" Hathor asked anxiously.

"There must be," she replied. "This joke is too elaborate for our hostess to have forgotten them." She found three sorts of cheese, a dish of butter, a bowl of mushrooms, and then, finally, a silver tureen filled with strawberries and cream. Hathor grabbed a ladle and began spooning the sweet mixture into his mouth.

Bith stood with her hands on her hips and surveyed the room. There was a sour expression on her face. "Someone is laughing at us," she said.

Cal raised a glass of wine. "To our kind hostess, wherever she is. May all her jests be so pleasant and may all her spells bring her whatever it is spells are supposed to bring." He downed the wine and smacked his lips.

"Sit down and eat, Bith," Endril said. He stuffed a

forkful of rabbit pie into his mouth. "The food is real enough, and it's wonderful."

"It just occurred to me," Bith said, "that if the food is here, then the bath may be here, too. I'm going upstairs."

There were four bedrooms, and one of them was clearly intended for a lady. A huge bed, draped in silk, dominated the room. There was also an elaborately decorated dressing table, a wardrobe, and, luxury of luxuries, a full-length mirror.

Bith stared at herself in the glass. She looked filthy and bedraggled. There was an unmistakable smear of dirt across her nose. "Talk about nightmares," she said to her reflection.

She opened the wardrobe. Inside, she found clothes, all suited to her size and taste. She pulled out an elegant dress, long and black, shot through with silver threads. "Lovely," she murmured. "But I can't get into it, as dirty as I am."

There was another door in the room. She had thought it led to the adjoining bedroom, but she found, instead, that it opened onto a tiny bathing room. In it was a tub filled with steaming water. Thick towels and cloths were piled beside it. Hastily, Bith disrobed and eased herself into the hot water. She scrubbed until her skin felt raw. When she saw how grey the water had turned, she shuddered.

I'm turning into a peasant, she thought. *With all this rough living, I'll soon be as coarse and ugly as Old Meg.* She examined her nails closely to make sure they were finally clean. *I think I'm ready to dress for dinner, now. I hope they've left me something—it would be just like those three to eat everything in sight.*

On the dressing table were bottles of scent, and in the drawers were elaborate hair clasps, brushes, and jewelry. Humming to herself, she slipped on the dress and put her hair up. This time, the reflection in the mirror was much more satisfying.

They've never seen me look like this, Bith thought happily. *Tonight, I do look like a princess.*

She descended the staircase slowly, and entered the dining room with a regal bearing. Cal, who was facing the hall, saw her first, and he was so startled he dropped his fork. Hathor and Endril turned. Hathor simply gasped, but Endril leapt to his feet and bowed. "Elizebith," he said, "you are lovely!"

Bith bowed her head slightly to acknowledge the compliment. She saw that her three friends were looking at each other with a certain amount of shame. "Perhaps you could excuse us for a few moments?" Endril asked her.

"Certainly."

She watched, amused, as they filed upstairs. When they were gone, she began to eat. The food was indeed excellent. She started wolfing down a piece of rabbit pie, then caught herself.

"Really, Elizebith," she scolded herself. "You've forgotten all your manners. Act like the lady you are." She began to eat slowly and daintily, as she had been taught.

Sitting in this congenial room, surrounded by comfort and luxury, she realized how much she missed the trappings of gentility and grace. Noticing that the room was becoming dark, she lit the tall slender candles that were on the table. As they began to burn, the room filled with the scents of beeswax and honey.

She reflected on how much of her life had been attended by custom and ritual. The life of any highborn lady was constrained by many rules of behavior, and the protocols and hierarchies she must observe could be as complex as the most intricate mathematical problem. But, added to that, was Bith's training as a magician, which bounded her life with constant ceremonial duties, disciplines, and observances.

Although she had often railed and rebelled against these strictures which took up so much of her time, they had also given her life a sense of stately order and purpose. She had missed this more than she knew. True, the unaccustomed freedom she had experienced since leaving her mother's house had been exhilarating. She did not wish to abandon her new life and go back to her old. Still, she was beginning to know herself well enough to realize that she would, someday, want to impose her own sense of order and discipline upon herself.

"Balance," she murmured. "Somewhere, there must be a balance between the two. I shall find it."

She heard footsteps and turned to see Endril, Hathor, and Cal coming back to dinner. As their faces had shown astonishment when she came into the room, so now did hers.

Cal looked every inch a young knight. His face, which she had always thought of as boyish, seemed more mature and experienced. His clothes, richly colored and textured, fitted him closely, showing off a body that was both strong and graceful. There was no hint of the sometimes gawky, sometimes rowdy, squire she knew. This was no longer Cal, but Caltus Talienson.

Hathor was dressed in clothes the color of the earth. Instead of looking ill-made and clumsy, with stumpy arms and legs, he looked powerful, elemental, like a being carved of stone. He moved slowly, but with assurance. Bith remembered his comment in Galen's Hearth about coming from a "very old troll family." For the first time, Bith wondered who Hathor was, among his own people. His stammering, broken speech and humble manner had always made her think of him as somewhat less than herself and the others. Now she felt ashamed for having taken him at his own silence.

Endril was dressed elegantly, in greys and browns—the colors of the forests he loved. With his lean body and sensitive face, he reminded Bith of some mysterious woodland creature—alien in many ways, unknowable to humans, sleek and swift, alive to scents and movements that eluded others.

What do I look like to them? Bith wondered.

Seated about the table, everyone's movements became stately and formal. There was little conversation, and the few words that were said, were spoken in low tones. They behaved as if any loud noise or abrupt movement would shatter something intangible yet precious.

After dinner, they went back to the main room and seated themselves. "This is so odd," Cal said. "I feel as if I were playing a role."

"Is the role completely foreign?" Endril asked.

"No," Cal said slowly. "It is simply that I've never behaved this well in my life." He laughed a bit. "I didn't eat my peas with a knife, I haven't teased Bith, and I haven't bragged about killing dragons. I don't even want to." He looked at Bith. "There would be no fun in calling you 'princess,' now. You look too much like one for there to be any jest in it. It would simply be calling you by the title you deserve."

"Indeed," Bith answered. "It is hard to believe I ever called you 'stableboy,' or that the name suited you. All of us seem transformed, or a part of us is revealed that was hidden before. Is this an enchantment?"

"I do not know," Endril replied. "Again, I feel no evil about, or any coercion of my will. Still"—and he sighed—"my impatience has not disappeared. My questions have not vanished. Our presence has been acknowledged, but where is the sorceress? How long must we wait until she shows herself? Is there a purpose to all this, or is it simply her way of showing hospitality?''

"Is like a story," Hathor said. "All of us look like people in stories. Act like it, too." He grinned. "Cal always eats peas with knife." He paused. "I usually use hands, except tonight."

"And how shall this tale end?" Bith asked. "Will we be accosted by dragons, or set upon by ogres? Shall Caltus save me from the monster? Or shall I be the maiden who tames the beast? Shall I wake to find a unicorn in my lap?" She laughed. "Are we truly in a tale such as those I read in my mother's house?"

"We cannot be," Endril said thoughtfully, "for we are still ourselves . . . even if on our best behavior and in our best clothes." He frowned. "Or someone's best clothes," he corrected himself.

"It is like being one of those tapestry figures, in a way," Bith said, gesturing toward the wall hangings. "We're a bit frozen in our noble gestures, with all the petty, everyday parts of us left out. It would get quite dull, and I couldn't keep it up forever."

On the mantelpiece stood a lap harp. It was gracefully wrought, and its wood was a warm, golden color. Endril picked it up and began to play. "In every story there is music," he said. "If nothing else, let us be true to our roles for one night."

Cal bowed to Bith and they began a slow dance called "The Lady Eleanor." They twirled about the room, Bith's long dress swirling about her, Cal's sword glinting in the firelight. Hathor's eyes followed them, and Bith broke away from Cal and pulled the troll to his feet. Hathor tried to follow her light steps and, surprisingly, he began to understand the rhythm. The slow beat suited his heavy bulk, and if it was not a graceful performance, neither was it an undignified one.

Finally, Endril put down the lap harp and he and Bith danced around the room, silently, using the memory of the tune as their guide. Their paces matched perfectly as they swept around the room, following the measures of the remembered melody.

They heard clapping. Standing in the door frame was Old Meg.

"You!" Bith said. "What are you doing here?"

"Why, I live here, my dear, when I feel like it," Old Meg replied.

Bith stared at her. "You're the sorceress? You're the one everybody's been talking about? I don't believe it!"

"Oh yes, it's me. Disappointed? Perhaps you were expecting someone a bit more . . . distinguished, shall we say?"

"At least someone a bit cleaner," Bith snapped back. "You could have at least bathed and changed your clothes."

"Ah, but this is a very faithful rendering of Old Meg, the seller of brooms and kindling. She always dressed like this and, I assure you, smelled just as bad, if not worse." The sorceress shuffled into the room, and gently eased herself into a chair, wincing a little. "She had rheumatism too—something dreadful it was. I wish I wasn't such a stickler for detail."

"What do you mean, *was*?" Endril asked. "And what, then, is your real name? And who is Old Meg?"

"Oho, Master Elf," she said, cackling. "You should know better than to ask a question like that. My name is not something I simply give out to just anyone. You may continue to call me Meg. It will serve. My real name— that's quite another matter."

She laughed again, rocking back and forth, her arms

clasped about her knees. "And it's very long—much too long for you to remember. It's still growing, too, I might add. Even my story's not done with, although I am quite ancient. No, Meg will do—short and easy and soon done with." Her laughter made her wheeze, and she stopped to catch her breath.

"Was there another Meg?" Cal asked, sounding bewildered.

"Oh, aye. Old Meg was the woman who lived in that hovel you so rudely allowed to be burnt down. I told you no untruths. . . . " She stopped, seeing the expressions on everyone's faces. "Very few, at any rate. She sold brooms and bits of kindling, rarely had enough to eat, had a husband who looked just like her, spent her days wandering this part of the mountains, and then, one day, she and he took sick and soon died—both of them."

"And you became Old Meg?" Cal asked. "Whatever for? And what were you to begin with?"

"To begin with, I was a being like yourself, or maybe it would be better to say, like our young lady here."

Bith's face expressed total disbelief. Meg grinned at her. "Hard to believe, I know. Well, I don't want to weary you with my life. It's such a long tale. Suffice it to say, I have been many things, and a young lady was not the most unlikely.

"At the time I met Old Meg, I was a tinker, and I was beginning to tire of it. And the time was coming when I must soon stop wandering. When she died, I thought she would make an excellent disguise. I let out that my husband had died but that I was fine. No one worries about an old beggar woman, eh?

"It's worked out well. People tell me all sorts of gossip. I never have outgrown my love for good stories. Besides, who would tell anything at all to a grand sorceress, except lies and flattery, if they thought they could get away with it?'' She glanced sharply at Bith. ''How long do you think it's been since Morea has heard anything but what's been shaped to please her?''

''What do you know about my mother?'' Bith demanded.

Meg leaned forward in her chair, but completely ignored Bith. ''I know them all down there. That John Sillar—what a rogue! Slaps my rump everytime he sees me!'' She broke into another cackle. ''Calls me his beauty, his swan. Knows a thing or two, though. He's seen many things in his years and he's wise to the ways of his fellows. It's always repaid me to listen to John Sillar. He's a wise fellow, as mortals go. But think of the story he's been missing all this time.''

''I don't believe you, you're lying!'' Bith shouted. She looked furious. ''I know something about being a sorceress, and you're a fraud. They aren't dirty and humpbacked and . . . and . . . how can someone like you know about my mother? You've heard stories somewhere, that's all.'' She looked to her friends for support. None of them said anything, but they all looked uncertainly at Meg, who looked right back at them. She seemed quite undisturbed by Bith's outburst.

''Not grand enough for you, am I, missy?'' She hobbled over to Bith, who backed away a pace. ''Not grand enough by half for any of you, I'll warrant.''

She peered into Cal's face. ''Old women don't figure in the romance you've made up for yourself, do they? No one sings brave songs about old crones and young knights—at least, not the sort of songs you'd want sung.'' She leered at him.

She stepped over to Endril. ''And you—oh, I know all about elves and their nobility, and the backside of it, which is their pride. No one but a beautiful sorceress, with slender arms as pale as moonlight and eyes that burn like stars, would do for you and your quest! Well, I'm past those vanities, even if you're not.'' She started to laugh again. ''I've acquired others.''

She turned to Hathor. ''As for you, my trollish friend, what did you hope for? Beauty again? But perhaps a bit more buxom than would please our elf. Elves like their women slender, but troll women are a nice handful, are they not?'' She jabbed Hathor in the ribs with one skinny elbow, and he jumped a foot.

She came back to Bith. ''I know what you want. And I've more to say to you than to the others—but it'll keep until tomorrow. I'll tell you this right now, though. That was a nice spot of magic you did up on the hill. Elementals are tricky little beasts.''

''How did you know about that?'' Bith asked.

''My dear, no one does magic so near my home that I don't know about it. I felt the earth give a little shake when you brought the creature up. No, you couldn't pull a coin from young Cal's nose without I'd know you'd done it— let alone what you really did do. A modest effort, but handled well, I say again. Didn't think you had it in you. And I enjoyed the fire very much.'' She grinned at Bith, showing off the brown stumps of teeth. ''I played the very same game when I was a girl. But I do think you were a bit hard on poor Meg, who never did you any harm!'' Her voice took on a cringing, pleading tone as she said this. Her grin grew wider.

Bith's mouth opened and then shut.

''Very wise, child. We learn the most when we are silent. And suffice it to say, my dears,'' Meg continued, addressing the four of them, ''that all of this''—she waved her hand about the room—''is my doing, and for your comfort. I hope my good dinner made amends for those beans I left in the hut. And you'll find the beds more comfortable than the dirt floor, I promise.''

"How did you know we were coming?" Cal asked. "Was it magic?"

"Oh, goodness no. John Sillar told me all about you. I saw you four ride off from the inn, and there's old John sitting there. What could be simpler and more natural than to hobble up and ask him? Strangers are always worth comment in these parts.''

"Bith says that using magic for something like conjuring up a dinner is wrong and wasteful,'' Cal said, challenging her. "But you say that's what you've done.''

Meg sighed. "This is the last question I'll answer tonight. Bith is quite correct—for Bith. She's a child still, and has no power to spare. Even the smallest act is, for her, a great drain. Furthermore, she was taught by someone, her mother, who is a highly skilled practitioner of her art but who, it could be argued, long ago lost all sense of proportion and any sense of humor she may once have had.

"I, on the other hand, have been practicing for many long years—far longer than Morea has been alive. I do not need to hoard my powers, as many others do. I have been stripped of many things to acquire this power—but I have no need to begrudge you your dinner.''

She rose. "We will talk more tomorrow. Conversation with mortals is very wearying. They ask so much, yet they learn so little. It's difficult to believe I was once one myself. I suggest you get some sleep.''

She hobbled to the door and stood there for a moment, framed by the night. She gave them an odd smile, almost wolfish, and her eyes seemed to glow for a moment. Then she was gone.

CHAPTER
6

They stared at the empty door frame.

"Incredible," Cal said, finally. "Is she really the sorceress?" he asked Bith.

"I suppose she must be," Bith answered. She shook her head in disbelief. "She's certainly played us for fools all around if she is."

"I believe her," Endril declared. "She's either the sorceress or the best liar I've ever met. She looks the same as when we met her at the hut, but all the cringing and subservience is gone. She acts very much like the mistress of this place. It's more flattering to ourselves to believe she's not what she claims, but all my feelings prompt me otherwise. What say you, Hathor?"

"Sharp elbows," Hathor muttered, rubbing his side. "Sharp tongue, also. Too bold, I think, to be lying."

"Then we accept her as the mysterious and powerful being we were looking for," Cal said. "If she is lying, I suppose it will come out soon enough. Only a great magician could help us. It's just that I wish she didn't look quite so much like an old scullery maid."

"It is disconcerting," Endril admitted. "I really did ex-

77

pect something more grand. In all the stories, she's described as tall and stately."

Bith snorted. "If what she says is true, she can look like anything she pleases. It could be worse, I suppose. Although I don't know how."

"She could have appeared as a sphinx or an ogre," Cal suggested. "That would have been worse."

"No, it wouldn't," Bith argued. "Then we wouldn't have been wondering about what she is. At least we'd know she was something uncanny. This way . . ." She broke off talking and yawned. "You know, I think I'll go to bed. We can argue about this till the cock crows and never come up with an answer. I suppose we'll find out something tomorrow. She has gall though, no matter what she turns out to be. I don't know when I've met anyone more irritating . . . except Vili."

"I too am weary," Endril said. "Perhaps we should retire."

"I just hoped she hasn't made the beds vanish," Cal grumbled as they went upstairs. "She seems to find amusement in the strangest things."

Bith's dream began with darkness illuminated by streaks of fire. Out of this darkness she saw a shadow form itself, until a blacker shape stood out against the night surrounding it. The shape moved and held out a hand. In it lay an ebony rock. Slowly, the hand closed about it, and a sense of weight and pressure began to build.

The air was thick with a smell of heat and charged with a feeling of imminent eruption. It was an atmosphere of suppressed hate, violence, and terror, seething and waiting for release.

The air burned white and, like a whirlpool, eddied around the shape. The hand clenched, and Bith doubled over with the unbearable pressure. Breathing was difficult, and she saw through a wash of red, as if anger had blinded her to all but itself.

Slowly, the tension relaxed. The fist unclenched. In its palm lay a crystal that glittered coldly in the darkness. Its light was shot through with the colors of the flame and white heat. She heard a deep laugh—mirthless, hollow, triumphant. There was a smell of smoldering ash.

She awoke to the sun pouring through her windows. After she dressed, she went downstairs and found her three friends already seated at the table. They were breakfasting on hot chocolate, rolls, and fruit.

Cal greeted her. "It's about time you woke up. I didn't want to leave you anything, but Endril made me. He told me I was a pig."

"Sounds like a fair description to me," Bith answered, pouring a cup of chocolate.

Endril studied her face. "Did you sleep poorly, Bith? You look tired."

"I had an odd dream. Did any of you dream last night?"

They shook their heads. "I don't remember a thing after my head touched that pillow," Cal said.

"Me too," Hathor said. "Sleep like the babies do."

"What did you dream?" Endril asked.

"Oh, I don't want to talk about it right now," Bith said, shrugging it off. "If that old biddy shows up again, she may have some answers. Frankly, I'd be just as happy if she stayed away."

"Old biddy, indeed! What kind of talk is that?" said Old Meg, coming into the room.

"If you made some noise coming into a room, like an ordinary person, we'd know not to talk about you when you're within hearing," Bith snapped.

"Oh, I like that," Meg answered, laughing a little.

"We are truly grateful for your hospitality," Endril said hastily. "You have been most gracious."

Meg waved her hand in a gesture of dismissal. "As I told you last night, it is no trouble. Indeed, I am flattered. It's been many a year since people came searching for me. Few believe in me at all anymore. Indeed, sometimes I can hardly believe in me myself." She emitted the high, dry cackle which seemed to be the only laugh she knew.

Bith listened to it carefully, and although it was rather grating, it was not the laugh she had heard in her dream the night before. It was irritating, but not menacing.

"Why did you come looking for me? How did you even know about me?" Meg asked.

"You are mentioned in several of our tales," Endril answered.

"Oh, of course. A great many years back I was quite close to your people. Those were the days when my interests were similar to theirs, and I was not so closely bound to this spot. And so they still believe in the old stories?"

"Some do, while others do not. I was unsure myself, but I felt I must try. There is so much to be done."

"What is this urgent matter?" Meg asked, idly buttering a roll.

"Surely you must know that this land is threatened by the Dark Lord, and that the Mistwall is very close?" There was surprise in Endril's voice.

"Oh yes, I have seen the Wall, but it has nothing to do with me."

"But you must want to drive it back!" Endril protested. "Your own home is threatened. It is a tool of the Dark Lord, and everything that comes from his hand is evil. And you know that his spies, the orcs, are close by."

"Hmmm . . . I do. Stupid, filthy creatures—why anyone

would use them, even as slaves, I can't understand.''

"I find your indifference in this matter quite incomprehensible," Endril declared. Although he tried not to show it, he was beginning to get angry.

"It's very simple—I am not threatened by any of this. It is purely a matter that concerns mortals. This house is a convenience I have constructed for you—nothing more. He cannot touch me. For me, the Dark Lord is like the shadow that falls across the moon—dark and mysterious but remote. I have long ago renounced my claims to the world of mortality and sensuality in which you are enmeshed."

She gazed into space for a moment. "Shadows pass, you know," she added. "They have their time, but are finally overcome by the light. And the light, too, has its seasons of ebb and flow . . .

"I'm sorry. I suppose you came here hoping for great things. When I was younger these issues interested me more, but now I'm content to leave these battles to others."

"You speak about this as if it were some sort of game," Cal said hotly. "We are fighting for our lives and the future of our world."

"But I tell you again that your world is not mine. You do not know what you are asking of me—it is not simply a matter of waving a wand and saying 'Shadows, begone!' You are appealing to me because you think we have common interests, but you are misled by my humble appearance. Really, there is very little resemblance between us any longer, beneath the skin."

"Nor am I human, nor is Hathor," Endril retorted. "Yet we have risked much in this struggle." His voice shook with anger.

"You have much to lose. You are not human, but you are mortal. A long life is granted to elves, but a finite one, for all that. It is certainly too short to let it be threatened by the Dark Lord. Your lands will be overrun, your existence reduced to one of abject slavery. Of course you fight—it is in your interests to do so. Were I you, death would be preferable to the Dark Lord's yoke—but I am not you."

"What are you, then?" Bith demanded. "You say you are not of us, yet my mother is flesh and blood, and she is a mighty sorceress."

"She may, in time, become like me. But I doubt if she will be exactly the same. There are choices we must make as we go further into our art. We lose some things to gain others. Morea has made her choices and her sacrifices. Now she begins to follow, to its end, the long path that is her destiny. My choices, and my path, have been different. And, as I told you, I am much older than Morea. I have traveled further along my road than she has on hers."

Meg pulled apart the roll she had buttered and began eating it. "I don't know why I bother with this," she muttered. "Eating is simply an old habit. I can't taste it." She crumbled the bread and dropped the pieces onto the floor.

She glanced up to see Bith looking at her with a rather shocked expression. "Oh, sorry, my dear. Table manners were never my strong suit . . . even when they mattered." She kicked the crumbs under the table.

"Now, where were we?" she asked, glancing around the table.

"You were explaining why you were too busy to help us," Cal said.

Meg gave him an amused glance. "Perhaps I can at least give you information. That costs me nothing, and will pass the time. Also, there are things Bith should know, if she does not already." ·

She looked over at Bith. "My dear, what has your mother explained to you about her clan?"

"Nothing at all. She's never said anything about any

kin.'' Bith looked embarrassed. ''I don't even know who my father is.''

''Oh, I don't mean blood ties. I mean her kin in magic—who she's aligned herself with.'' Seeing Bith's look of confusion, Meg said, ''Never told you a thing, I see. I suspected as much. I suppose it falls to me.'' She sighed. ''I never enjoyed this.

''Now, Bith, these are things rightly said by your teacher—whoever's bringing you up in the art. In your case, it would be Morea. However, I think I'll break with the rule and tell you myself. It may make some things clearer to you, and perhaps to your friends, also.''

Meg stared at the ceiling for a moment, her lips pursed. ''At some point,'' she began, ''after they've gotten well into their studies and have shown true promise, aspiring magicians either join a clan of like-minded folk, or else they abandon their calling. It may surprise you to know that that's what most do—give it up.''

Bith looked unconvinced. ''Why would anyone do that?—especially after working so hard.''

''Because, until that time, they gave little and received much.'' Bith opened her mouth and started to object. Meg held up a hand to silence her.

''I know, you think you've made all sorts of sacrifices—fastings and vigils, ceremonies and countless hours given to study. Pooh! Children learning their lessons do as much. But to go further, you must prove your worth and your mettle, and I promise you, the proofs are hard. The power of a great magus is not bought cheaply. Many will not pay that price.

''Most who turn away, turn away completely. Often their lives are troubled and sad, for they suffer from a hunger which they themselves cultivated but now can never satisfy.'' Meg sighed. ''If I had pity left in me it would be for them. And also, I would honor them, for they have made a hard, bitter choice.

"A few keep on in a small way. They may become healers and sellers of potions. Others, acting, I believe, out of anger, become conjurors and performers. They wish to demean the knowledge they were forced to renounce.

"Lastly are those I understand the least. They are the ones who walk away and never look back. Somehow, they continue their lives as ordinary folk, surprisingly free of resentment or regret. I could never have done that."

Bith shifted uneasily in her chair. "What happens if you don't want to give it up?"

"You must join one of the clans—there are only a few. Usually, although not always, students join the same clans as their teachers. They must, of course, pass a rather severe test." Meg cleared her throat and looked a bit nervous.

"What sort of test?" Bith asked suspiciously.

"Oh, summoning some sort of power and having it perform some act. That's typically what they do. It has to be something significant but not impossible."

"What happens if you fail?" Cal asked. "Do you get another chance?"

"No, there's only one chance. Now, after the test . . . "

"You haven't answered the first part of Cal's question," Endril interrupted. "What happens if you fail?"

"Don't all pester me at once," Meg snapped. "I'm getting to it." She smoothed out some wrinkles in the tablecloth and rearranged the bread and rolls into a neat pile. "I believe I shall keep company only with trolls," she said rather sulkily. "They know how to keep still.

"As I was saying," she continued, "the tests are difficult and, quite often, if you fail, you die. The creatures you must summon are rather ill-tempered, you know. If they find you can't control them, they tend to turn on you. Not always," she added hastily, seeing the expression on everyone's face, "but quite often." She shrugged. "That's the way of it—a messy business, really."

"You're well out of this," Cal said to Bith. "I can't believe your own mother would let you become involved in something so dreadful."

Bith said nothing. She stared at the floor, her face thoughtful.

"You know I'm right, don't you?" he insisted, pressing her for an answer.

"No, I don't."

"You're being stubborn," he said angrily. "What would you do—risk your life so you can become like her?"

Meg tittered. "Don't insult your hostess, my boy. It's not mannerly."

"You risk your life, Cal," Bith said. "The battle you and Sir Edric were in—that was going to make you a knight if you did well. You were ready to sacrifice your life for that. Why should it be any different for me?"

"It is different, that's why! Being a knight means being willing to die for a noble cause," Cal argued. "It's not the same thing at all!" His face was flushed. He had the uncomfortable feeling he wasn't making any sense.

"You agree with me, don't you?" he asked, appealing to Endril.

Endril looked troubled. His answer came slowly, as though he were forcing the words from his mouth. "No, I must agree with Bith. She is right, I think, although I would never wish harm to come to her. I cannot tell whether her risk would be worth the gain. Each of us must decide that for ourselves, no matter what our quest."

"Tell me more," Bith said to Meg. "Should you pass the test, what happens?"

"More study, greater knowledge, more power, and—

hopefully—more wisdom. There will be other tests of increasing difficulty, although not necessarily so dangerous to life itself. Many fail these tests, but survive. They continue as magicians, but their knowledge grows no greater. They have reached their proper level. The greatest become members of the governing council, and the greatest of these leads it.''

"What are these clans you speak of?" Endril asked. "I had not known of them."

"Ah, now we're getting to an interesting story. In telling you of the clans, I shall also tell you of the Dark Lord's beginnings," Meg answered.

"Now, there are three clans—two of them closely related and friendly, and one of them a group of renegades. You can guess which of them the Dark Lord belongs to. He is the head of it, in fact.

"But long, long ago, even before my time, there was only a single group of magicians. They worked and studied together. Their aims were, I suppose, noble. They wanted knowledge of a certain kind, and by knowledge they meant understanding and wisdom, too.

"Of course, there began to be problems. One group wanted to go one way, and others argued for a different path. At first, it wasn't too serious. Some of them were very interested in the natural world—forests, mountains, oceans, the beings that inhabited them, and the invisible web that bound it all together. Others were more interested in ideas and forms. They sought for permanence beneath the shifting tides of the world. The two groups complemented each other, when you think of it.

"As time passed, the rivalry increased. There was jealousy and dissension. Instead of seeing each side as a part of the whole, each side began to insist they *were* the whole and the other side was made up of fools or incompetents.

"At a time when the enmity was very great, a student came along who was exceptionally gifted. He mastered each level with an ease that was astounding. Everyone expected great things of him, for not only was he gifted, he was forceful and persuasive. Also, he had ambition, possessed an iron will and the courage of a lion. A formidable man, all the way around. He was asked to choose between the two disciplines, but he refused. He said there should be a way to reconcile them, and he would find that way.

"Many were hopeful he would succeed. The doors of learning were opened to him fully, and he mastered the secrets of both houses. Great things were expected."

Meg sighed. "Unfortunately, they never happened. The student's love of power, and his ambition, coupled with his great abilities, overmastered him. Fascination with the world, and the rules that governed it, led to a desire for control. The search for ideals bred a coldness that quickly became cruelty. His ambition turned to ruthlessness. His great talents only made him contemptuous of others.

"It was a dreadful business. Several magicians were seduced by his achievements and promises of further glory. He could offer very concrete rewards to those who would follow him.

"These sorcerers became the founders of the third group, and he heads their council. As you well know, they have come far in their own quest. They have conquered and enslaved, and wield great power in this life. Others have followed in the path they laid out."

"It is strange," Endril mused. "I had thought of him existing always as he is now. The idea of him changing, of once being something other than a monster, never occurred to me."

"Ah, there you make a a great mistake," Meg said. "Powerful as he is, he is not omnipotent. He has limitations and is bound by laws and rules, as are we all. Nor is he immune to change and the great currents of ascendance and decay that govern the world.

"Also, many of his servants are mortal creatures, such as you are yourselves. Have you not killed orcs, and bested other servants of his?" She chuckled. "John Sillar had many tales to tell me of the heroes of Cairngorm."

Cal groaned.

"Vili has told us of an amulet that is now in the Dark Lord's possession," Endril ventured. "It controls dreams, Vili said, and can give them substance. All of us have felt its effects, and if you have talked to Sillar, you must know that all the villagers have been disturbed by it. Can you tell us anything of this charm?"

Meg looked thoughtful. "I can, indeed. It was lost for uncounted years. It seems it has been found again."

"I think I know something of it," Bith said quietly.

They all turned to look at her.

"Last night, I dreamed I was present when it was created. At least, I think that's what I saw." She looked at Meg. "Is it a crystal, small enough to be held in the palm of the hand? Does it give off a light of its own—cold as ice, yet shot through with the colors of fire?"

Meg nodded. "It does. Tell us of your dream."

Bith recounted her dream of the night before. She tried to describe the sense of suffocation she had suffered. "I was not simply a bystander," she said. "I was somehow the stone, and endured the heat and pressure.

"At the same time, I was he who created the stone." She shuddered. "I have never experienced such desolation of the spirit. It was what I imagine it to be like at the heart of a volcano that is close to eruption. I felt suffocated by feelings of rage, anger, and hate.

"Finally, the pressure stopped and, in his palm, lay the

crystal, as I have described it to you. Then he laughed.''
She shivered again. ''It was a triumphant laugh, but a cruel
one, also. There was no joy in it.

''What does it mean?'' Bith asked Meg. ''Why did I have
this dream when no one else dreamt at all?''

Meg studied her closely. ''I think I might know. But first,
let me tell you the story of this crystal.

''The Dark Lord had cast his lot with the world, and his
magic is tied to its objects. I, for instance, no longer have
need of wands and charms and baubles. That is because I
have severed my relations with this plane of life. I neither
suffer from its penalties, nor do I enjoy its great gifts.''

She gestured in a broad, sweeping movement that en-
compassed her guests, her home, and all that lay beyond.
''None of this seems very real to me. It is as though I were
watching you through a glass, or as if you were at the bottom
of a clear pool, and the water, shifting and distracting, made
it impossible to see you clearly. It is all quite dreamlike. It
was not always so.'' Meg lapsed into silence. She seemed
to have forgotten they were there.

Endril cleared his throat. ''You were telling us about the
crystal,'' he said rather loudly.

''What?'' she asked, her voice sharp. She looked around.
''Are you still here? What do you want?'' Her voice sounded
querulous.

''You were explaining the difference between your magic
and the Dark Lord's,'' Bith said impatiently. ''Don't you
remember?''

Meg shook her head, as if to clear it. ''Sorry, my dears.
I was thinking of something else. I'll get on with it.

''The Dark Lord is wise in his own way. Once his council
was formed, he looked for a way to keep it under control.
He knew with a certainty that just as he had rebelled against
his masters, so would his own captains someday rebel

against him. He wanted to put a stop to it before it started.

"All his followers had come to his side because they were driven by lust—for power, for wealth, for revenge. It occurred to him that if he could forge a weapon which would control these feelings, he could control his followers, forever.

"Deep in the pits of the earth he worked his magic. He wrought a crystal from blackest stone. A demon, a haunter of dreams and a bringer of nightmares, was conjured up and, spitting like a cat, imprisoned within it. The Dark Lord called the crystal the Dreamstone, and hung it round his neck with a silver chain.

"With this stone he controlled his followers, sending phantoms to seduce them, and twisting their emotions, bending them to his will. They, who had so longed for domination, were really his slaves.

"As the Dark Lord's power increased and his ascendancy grew, the peoples of the earth fought mighty battles against him and his minions. Many died, and songs are still sung of those times. The councils of the two clans elected to destroy the Dark Lord if they could, or if they could not, at least destroy his tools—his amulets and charms—and weaken him. For that is a penalty of being so tied to the things of the earth—its objects are vulnerable. They can be lost, or stolen, or destroyed. Without them, the power they hold can no longer be wielded.

"So, one of the council members went in search of him. She was not the oldest member, nor the most skilled, but she had courage, and a great love of the earth's beauty. To see it destroyed was more than she could bear. She was the one most driven by the desire to help."

"Was it you?" Endril asked.

Meg nodded. "It was, indeed. How distant it all seems. Much has changed since then. And I have changed most of all.'' She sighed, and fell silent for a moment, reflecting on that distant past.

"It was a terrible journey,'' she continued. "The smell of burning, of charred flesh, never left my nostrils. It seemed as if all the world were running with anguish and darkness— a great sore that would never be healed.

"I remember always being thirsty and never having enough to eat. In those days, I still needed the earth to sustain me, and I suffered with the rest of her children. There was an endless, dangerous trek over cruel mountains. I barely avoided capture. By the time I reached his home, I was already greatly weakened.

"At that time, he housed himself in a high tower where he could overlook the waste that was his domain. Before I dared venture in, I kept vigil for several days at its base— hidden by spells from the eyes of his many watchers.

"He sensed me. He knew I was somewhere near, but he could not find me. Cloaked in his own shadows, his eye tried to pierce the darkness he himself had created, looking for the enemy crouched in his most secret domain.

"Finally, I began the weary climb to the tower's upper room. All was quiet—I met no one. I knew he was waiting for me. He was daring me to confront him. I hoped that his arrogance would be his undoing.

"As I've said, I was already weak. I did not believe I could kill him. I determined to do as much damage as I could before I died.''

"Were you so certain of death?'' Endril asked.

"I had no hopes, and yet, death was my best hope. Desire for aught else did not survive in such a place.

"In the end, it was my weakness that saved me. As I entered the chamber, I remember him standing there—a towering shape, cloaked in a mist that swirled about him, hiding his body from my sight. Two red eyes stared at me, glittering like rubies on black velvet.

"He laughed when he saw me, and beckoned for me to come to him. And I wanted to . . . so, so badly. He pulled me toward him the way a magnet pulls iron. I yearned for those arms to fold about me and cloak me in darkness, with him, forever.

"I dared not come closer. I felt my will crumble before his. Instead of approaching, I saw a glowing orb on a table, and I took it and smashed it. He screamed when it shattered on the floor.

"Everything there, you see, contained a piece of him, to some degree or another. It was the only way I could wound him. He grabbed me then. We grappled and he pressed me close. There was a smell of cold ash, yet my body burned . . . I could not pull loose, and his eyes were like bores, going ever deeper into me.

"I felt something pressing against my chest, and my hand closed around it. It seared my palm like a burning coal. It was the Dreamstone. With what little will I had left I used a spell to augment my strength. I yanked on the chain and it broke. I threw the thing away from me and it went out the window.

"In his anger, he lifted me up and hurled me from the tower. I remember falling, and a terrible pain, and then, nothing."

There was a long silence. Outside, a bird was singing. Finally, Bith asked, "What happened to you afterward?"

Meg sighed. "I was found and brought back to my clan. An army of mortals, and magicians, came hard upon my heels. I was cared for, but it could never be the same afterward. I renounced the world and my body. I follow different ways now.

"The Dark Lord was beaten back, as you all know. He

fled and lay quiet for many, many years. We preferred to think he was gone and the danger over. It was foolish. He is stirring again, it seems, although he is far more cautious than in his younger days."

She turned to Bith. "As to your earlier question, about your dream—I think you dreamt as you did because the crystal has been found, and he is using it to bring his servants back to him."

She touched Bith's face gently with one finger. "You look so much like your mother. She is a member of his clan, you know. I believe that you, as her daughter and pupil, are sensitive to the dreams he uses to call his people back to him."

"No!" Bith stood up abruptly, tipping over her chair. "I want no part of it!" She ran out of the house, weeping.

CHAPTER
7

Bith ran into the orchard, tears streaming down her face. "I'm cursed," she wept. She leaned against a tree, her back to the world, and tried to stop the tears. "Stupid," she said, kicking the tree. "Stop it, stop crying."

"Whatever is the matter, dear?"

Bith turned to see Meg standing there.

"What do you think is wrong?" Bith retorted. "Do you think I enjoy getting these dreams? Do you think I want to be trapped into kinship with the Dark Lord? I didn't ask for any of this. It's not fair!"

"Let me help you, Bith. I can, you know. I have great power."

Bith looked at Meg, studying her face. It seemed kindly and gentle. *But it's not hers*, Bith thought. *It's a face she's only borrowed. What is her true face?*

"Come with me, Bith, and I'll help you." Meg touched her gently on the shoulder.

"Come with you where?" Bith asked. "How can you help me?"

"I can free you from this taint. I can stop the dreams. I can offer you haven. Is that not what you wish?"

"I . . . yes . . . but I can't leave my friends."

"You shall not desert them. You will have great power. You shall be better able to aid them in their quest. Knowledge will be yours and the will to use it. Nothing shall stand before you."

Meg took hold of Bith's wrist. "Come with me!"

Bith started. Meg's voice had changed. It sounded harsher and more demanding. Her hand felt cold, wooden.

"Let me go," Bith demanded. She tried to yank away.

Meg's grip became tighter. Her face crumpled and began re-forming. The bent, old body straightened and lengthened. Schlein, his face scarred, stood there, holding Bith fast. Around his neck hung the Dreamstone. "Come with me!" he said again. He began to laugh. His mouth grew wider and wider until his entire face disappeared into a black cavern. Bith was too terrified to scream.

"Get thee gone from this place!" someone called out. "False image—how dare you trespass! Begone or suffer my wrath!"

Bith looked over her shoulder. Meg was there. She looked furious. Her whole face was contorted with rage. Cal, Hathor, and Endril were running toward her. Bith cried out, "Help me!"

Meg pointed her finger at Schlein. There was a scream and a sound like glass shattering. The image flickered and vanished. There was a sound of air rushing in, then there was silence. The impress of Schlein's fingers stood out starkly around Bith's wrist.

"Bith, are you all right?" Cal asked, running up to her. She nodded, unable to speak.

"The greedy, interfering fool," Meg spat out. She stamped the ground with one foot. "How dare he trespass . . . how dare he . . . " She stopped. "Who was that meddling amateur?"

"His name is Schlein," Endril answered. "He is a servant of the Dark Lord. He wields the crystal in lieu of his master."

"I cannot believe he did this under orders," Meg protested. "I tasted his hatred . . . it was his own."

"He holds many grudges against Bith," Endril answered. "She has thwarted him again and again. He desires her and she spurns him. He has suffered bodily harm because of her. She has made him look a fool."

"So he uses the stone for his personal revenge," Meg said thoughtfully. "That is very interesting. He is in a vulnerable place. The Dreamstone is overmastering him. Once his servant is destroyed, the Dark Lord will take it back, perhaps to wield it himself. If you truly want to find it, now is the time."

She looked at the four friends, her glance keen and penetrating. "Go back to the house," she ordered. "I will meet you there before night."

"But . . . " Endril started to say.

She held up a hand, silencing him. "Please, no arguments. I've no patience for the dithering of mortals. Either return to the house and wait, or leave. It is up to you. Frankly, I'd prefer that you leave. I do not look forward to another tangle with the Dark Lord, or his wretched servants."

She turned her back on them and walked away. Cal started to go after her, but Endril held him back.

"Let's return to the house," he said resignedly. "It seems our portion is obedience and patience."

The day crept by and still Meg did not appear. Endril, Hathor, Cal, and Bith all stayed in the house, waiting, restlessly walking through the rooms, opening cupboards, and staring out the window, watching the sun climb high into the sky and then tracing its slow descent to the horizon.

The house itself was a lonely place. It was plain to them it had never been lived in. Aside from the furnishings and clothes they had found, there was nothing there. The bookshelves were bare, and there was not a single one of the thousand unnecessary things that clutter up a house and make it into a home.

It had less comfort than an inn. Although the walls were substantial and the doors made a noise when they shut, there was a feeling of impermanence about the place—as if it could disappear with a strong puff of wind. It made them all uneasy. It made them feel like ghosts.

"Enough of this waiting! I say we go after them," Cal declared, bringing his fist down on the table.

"Go after whom, exactly?" Endril asked.

"Them . . . Schlein and his gang . . . we can't let them go on using the stone."

"Go where, though?" queried Hathor. "Could be anywhere." He ran a finger gently along the blade of his axe. "Would like to fight, but how fight dreams?" He looked at Cal questioningly.

"I've got it all figured out," Cal answered. "We follow the orcs' trail. We'll go back to the hut and pick up the trail from there. It shouldn't be hard. We'll follow it back to Schlein, take the crystal from him, and kill him. That's something we should have done long ago."

"It would be a very old trail," Endril countered. "They're almost two days ahead of us, and that's a great deal. Orcs are swift and hardy travelers. Also, they're sure to have brought back some tale. It would seem from Bith's vision that Schlein knows where we are. But we do not know where he is. I don't know how close you have to be for the Dreamstone to work, or if distance matters at all.

There is so much I do not understand—perhaps it would be wisest to wait for Meg.''

"Magic!" Cal snorted. "I'm tired of it! There's no substitute for a good, sharp broadsword to my way of thinking. Some straightforward mayhem would be a relief after all this talk and sorcery.''

He looked at Bith. "How are you feeling, princess? Better?''

"Confused, disturbed, unhappy, worried," she said, ticking each word off on a finger. "I suppose that means I feel fine." She smiled.

"What do you think we should do?" Endril asked her. "You are the one most threatened.''

"Let's wait for Meg. I think she truly means to help us. Surely we'll be better off with her than without?" Bith looked questioningly at her companions.

"Can't leave without more food," Hathor pointed out. "Finished everything she gave us. No good hunting orcs if have no way to stay alive.''

"I suppose that's true," Cal admitted reluctantly. "At least we can get that from Meg. She seems to be able to conjure up anything she wants. It's eerie. I wish she'd hurry, though. The day's drawing on and she said she'd be here before night. It's almost that now. What will we do if she doesn't come?''

"Then we're back where we started," Endril said. "We'll have to go back to town and decide what to do next. It doesn't bear thinking about. I hope she gets here soon. I, too, am weary of waiting. It's how we've spent most of our time.''

"Getting restless, are you, dearies?" Meg said, coming into the room.

"We were wondering what happened to you," Cal said. "Where have you been?''

"Walking and thinking. Thinking and walking."

"That's useful," he retorted. "How are you going to help us?"

"What do you want to do?"

"Get the Dreamstone and destroy it," Bith answered.

"Ah, I think that is a little too ambitious, Elizebith. It is filled with the Dark Lord's power. Until he meets his end, I do not think it can be destroyed."

"You could do it—you said you destroyed one of his objects."

"It was far more fragile than the Dreamstone. Even now, I doubt that I could destroy it. Although my power has grown since those days, so has his. He has not spent these many years slumbering."

"I hate magicians—they find it impossible to give simple answers," Cal said. "Why can't you just say, 'Good idea, I'll do it for you'? No. Instead 'It's a long story', or 'His power has grown.' Always excuses and qualifications. I'm tired of it! I want plain answers and simple solutions."

Meg laughed. "So do we all, but we rarely get them."

"If you can't destroy the stone, what can you do?" Endril asked. He struggled to mask his impatience. "We have traveled far and are weary. Inaction and uncertainty are hard to bear. Give us your best advice—if that is all you have to give—provision us, and let us be on our way. We can at least track down the rest of the orcs, as Cal suggests."

"It is dark," Meg said. "It would be unwise to leave tonight. Stay here one more night, and tomorrow your way will be clearer. I will help you find it. I promise."

Endril sighed. He looked worried and unhappy. "Do we have another choice?" he asked his friends. "Every hour we delay, the trail gets colder, yet to hunt them during the night seems foolish. The way is treacherous and our path uncertain. I doubt if we could find the hut, in the darkness."

He looked to each of them, awaiting an answer.

"One more night," Cal said. He looked disgusted.

Hathor nodded his agreement.

"I suppose we stay," Bith said. She too sounded unhappy. "But I do not relish another night in this place. I fear what dreams sleep will bring me."

"We learn much from those dreams," Meg said.

"Nothing that was not already known," Bith objected. "You could have told us about the stone's origins."

"We learned something more important than that. We have learned that you can see the Dreamstone. I assure you, that is very rare. We have also learned that this Schlein, as you call him, is using it to reach you. He is guiding you to it. What could be better, if you truly wish to find it?"

"If I do find it, and capture it, can I make it my own? It would be a fearsome weapon against the Dark Lord, and a fine irony to use his own tools against him."

"If you find it, I suggest you get rid of it. You could not control it—it would control you. It was made with evil intent by a great master. Even this Schlein, who is far more practiced than yourself, crumbles before it. Do you truly think you could be its ruler?" Meg gave her a searching look.

Bith shifted her eyes. "No, I suppose not. Then, what should I do with it?"

"Throw it off the highest peak, or into the deepest river. I favor the river, myself. Free flowing water is a great purifier. But keep it no longer than you must, for it is perilous."

"It sounds like a hollow victory," Cal said. "If we cannot destroy it, why should we not use this thing for our own purposes? We are not evil as the Dark Lord is."

"Are you so certain of yourself?" Meg asked him. "Are you so sure of your purity and selflessness? Have you never had a base thought or an evil wish? Has anger or hatred never overwhelmed you, even for a moment? Have you never yielded to temptation?''

''I didn't say I was perfect,'' Cal muttered.

''Then do not toy with such foolish ideas. The very fact that the stone has shaped your dreams means you are vulnerable to its allure. Use it and you will be the Dark Lord's.''

''Always bad news,'' Hathor said.

''I will leave you to yourselves tonight,'' Meg said. ''Prepare for the morrow. There will, I promise you, be changes.''

Bith was in a cave with long, winding passages. She was lost. The walls glowed with an eerie green light, and she crept along cautiously. She could not remember why she had come to this place. It seemed that she had been wandering here all her life, with no hope of rest. There had never been anything but these rocky walls and cold, damp air. Sunshine and light belonged to another world. That they existed she accepted as a fact, but one that had no bearing on her.

Ahead of her was the sound of water falling. As she came closer, the noise became a roar and the air was filled with a heavy mist. The cave opened out onto a ledge and she stood on one side of a chasm. On the other side, a cataract tumbled down the mountainside into a foaming river far, far below.

I'm supposed to do something, she thought. *But what? It was something important. . . .*

She walked out onto the ledge and stared down. The river twisted and foamed and leapt like a living being. The white-capped waves seemed to scrabble at the air, as if to free themselves, and then subsided into the water's body.

Fascinated, she bent over to see more clearly. Her foot slipped out from under her and she teetered back and forth on the edge. She tried to regain her balance but couldn't. She tumbled off the ledge.

Her fall seemed to happen very slowly. As she fell, she noticed the different shades of grey and brown that colored the mountain's flanks. Here and there, she saw the dull glitter of a vein of ore or some moss growing against a rock. A clump of flowers with violet petals and delicate green leaves caught her attention. As she passed them, the air filled with their heady scent. She wondered, idly, if she would fall forever.

Glancing down, she saw the water beneath her, and the boulders, scattered like teeth, in the riverbed. The whitecaps reached up, eager to embrace her. She started to scream. Her cry echoed in the chasm.

Bith sat up, her eyes wide, her mouth still open. Cal's nose was an inch from hers. "Get your face out of my face," she snapped, brushing hair from her eyes.

"I was just trying to rouse you," Cal grumbled, "before you screamed yourself awake. Take a look around. Then you'll really start screaming."

"What . . . why . . . where??" Bith spluttered.

She was sitting on the ground. The four walls and ceiling of the house she'd slept in had been replaced by the open air. The house had completely disappeared. The land was as desolate and bare as anything they'd seen outside the valley. Gone were the garden and fruit trees. The lush grass was replaced by brittle sedge and rock.

"I was the first to waken," Endril said. "This is what greeted me when I opened my eyes." He waved his hand in a gesture of disgust. "We've been had."

"Didn't even leave us food," Hathor said.

"Nothing?" Cal asked anxiously. He started looking around.

"Even looked under rocks," Hathor responded glumly. "Nasty old woman."

Bith got to her feet. "Have you noticed that we're in our clothes? I don't know about you, but I distinctly remember putting on my shirt before I got into bed. Now I'm in the dress I wore yesterday. What sort of joke is this?" She began brushing off dust and bits of gravel from the black dress.

"All our belongings are in that pile," Endril said, pointing to a jumbled heap a few yards off. But this is no joke— we're in serious trouble. I don't see the horses anywhere."

Bith gasped. "How will we get back?"

"Shank's mare, princess," Cal answered. "We walk."

"We'll never be able to do it."

"It will be a weary journey, and we have no food," Endril said, "but it can be done. We know where to find water at least." He shrugged. "What choice have we?"

"Why would she do this?" Bith asked. "If she doesn't want to help us, I suppose it is her choice, yet she spoke as though she'd decided to do something. To simply abandon us like this and take the horses to boot—it seems like simple malice."

"Probably took horses to eat," Hathor muttered.

"Will you stop talking about eating?" Bith said irritably. "I'm hungry enough without you harping on the notion. Besides, that's a disgusting thing to say."

"Horses not disgusting. Before I changed mind about flesh, had eaten many times. Good."

"That's enough, Hathor," Endril said. "We'll discuss it another day."

"Maybe Meg really wasn't the sorceress," Cal suggested.

"Perhaps she was just some sort of thief who took advantage of us. We never really saw her do anything magical, did we?''

''I don't think you're right, Cal,'' Endril said. ''She was too sure of herself, and she knew too much. Besides, she did cause the image of Schlein to vanish.''

''How do we know that? Maybe it was just a coincidence. All she did was point her finger.''

''How do you explain the house?'' Bith asked.

''We've no proof it was her doing. Did you see her wave her arms and say 'House, begone!'? Maybe we've never met the real sorceress. Meg's a fake and she got away from us just in time. The real sorceress wondered what we were doing in her house. This is her punishment for tresspass-ing.''

''Far too many coincidences, Cal,'' Endril pointed out. ''For someone who likes simple explanations, yours is as tortured as any I've ever heard. It's much simpler to believe Meg is, indeed, the sorceress, and that she'd decided we're not worth her time. She said herself that none of this really mattered to her, that we barely seemed real to her. I just wish she'd given us some food and left us the horses.'' He sighed. ''All this is vain speculation. It matters not a whit what she is or isn't. It won't solve our problem for us.''

He looked at his companions. They saw how troubled his face was. ''I beg the pardon of all of you,'' he said. ''This quest was at my urging. I have failed, not only in my search, but in my duty to you. This fiasco is my fault.''

''Don't blame yourself, Endril,'' Cal said, clapping him on the shoulder. ''You had no way of knowing what a treacherous old hag she'd be. You did your best. When you get back to your people, just make sure they change those old stories about the sorceress of Mount Thalia.''

Hathor and Bith nodded. ''Really, Endril,'' Bith said, ''none of us blame you. We came of our free will. All of us had a chance to leave, but none of us wanted to.''

"Should start," Hathor said. "Sooner begin, sooner arrive at Galen's." He began shouldering the packs.

"I never thought I'd say this," Bith said, picking up her things, "but I'll wager by the time we get to that inn, I'll be weeping tears of joy. I'll give every flea a kiss." She shuddered.

"Are we ready?" Cal asked.

"Just a moment," Bith said.

"Meg!" she shouted. "I hope you can hear me. You're a disgrace to your art and your kind. Oathbreaker, may your powers wither, may your spells go awry, may your demons mock you! Let this curse follow you till the sands of this world are washed away and the light of the stars has waned." With great solemnity, she spat.

"I'm ready," she said.

They trudged back the way they had come. Before they had gone too far, Endril stopped and sniffed the air.

"What is it?" asked Cal.

"I smell air that is cool and wet—I smell water and darkness."

"How can anyone smell darkness?" Bith demanded. She sat down wearily on a rock. "My feet hurt," she complained.

"Air that springs from a dark place, then—a cavern. Stop quibbling, Bith, I'm not in the mood. I do not remember this, yet I am sure we are following the same path as before."

"Is important?" Hathor asked.

"Oh, probably," Bith answered, flatly and without enthusiasm. They all looked at her and she recounted her latest dream.

"I search," Hathor said. "Bith's dreams always mean something. Which way is smell?"

Endril pointed to a tumble of rocks at the base of a slope. "From that direction, I think."

Hathor began picking up boulders and hurling them out of the way. "We see what there is to see."

"I'll help you," Cal said. He struggled to pick up one of the stones, but dropped it abruptly, with a grunt. Slowly, painfully, he straightened up.

"Good job, Hathor," he said approvingly. "Try a little over to the right."

"I see hole," Hathor shouted. He was rocking a large boulder back and forth, struggling to dislodge it.

They all rushed over and began to push. The rock rolled away and revealed a cave. The odor of dank air was unmistakable.

Bith's heart lurched. Staring into the gloomy interior, she wished she were anywhere but where she was.

"Well, does it remind you of the place you dreamed about?" Cal asked impatiently.

She nodded. "This is it—I feel it in my bones. I know the Dreamstone is in there, someplace. Do we have to go in?"

"You don't have to, princess, but I'm definitely going in. I'd feel like an awful coward if I ran away now."

"Perhaps our discovery of this cave means Meg is helping us," Endril suggested.

"If this is her notion of help," Bith said, "then I'd gladly do without, thank you."

She smiled sweetly at Cal and curtseyed. "After you."

CHAPTER
8

The cave was as she remembered it from her dream. The walls glowed with a dull luminescence and there was the endless sound of dripping water. They moved slowly, in single file, openly sighing with relief as hulking shadows resolved themselves into formations of rock or dissolved into patterns of light and gloom.

"This is a really pointless expedition if the only thing that's going to happen is I fall off a ledge and die," Bith said.

"You won't slip and you won't die," Cal assured her. He took her hand. "We're here with you. You were alone in the dream."

Bith squeezed his hand in a gesture of gratitude.

The cavern began to widen, and they found themselves walking through massive chambers whose ceilings vaulted high above them. Stalactites hung like daggers, and the walls glittered with water droplets and the veins of ore that laced themselves through the rock. The air was getting colder.

Occasionally, they saw pools of water. In them, eyeless fish, with feelers, swam about. Clumps of bats hanging from the ceiling, disturbed by the intruders, would swoop above them, looking for new resting places.

"I don't like this place," Bith muttered through gritted teeth.

"Do you have any notion of where to find the Dreamstone, Bith?" Endril asked.

She shook her head. "I have a premonition that it will find us. I can hardly wait."

"Stop, everyone," Endril commanded. "Something's wrong."

Cal's hand went to his sword pommel. "What is it?"

"Listen," Bith whispered. "There's something moving, ahead of us."

They strained to catch any noise. Gradually, increasing in volume as it drew closer, came a sound of shuffling and grunting.

"Get behind these rocks," Endril directed. "Get out of sight."

They hid, trembling, waiting for this unknown danger to appear. The air grew strong with the rank smell of an animal. A misshapen shadow loomed on the wall.

Their eyes widened in disbelief. Though they could not speak, their thoughts were the same: *This cannot be—it is another dream.*

A Cyclops slouched into view. It was larger than the largest bear, and seemed an obscene mixture of human and animal. Although it walked upright, it was shaggy with hair. Its hands were a man's hands, but the fingers ended in long, filthy claws.

The beast stopped to snuffle the air, and its single eye rolled about in its head, looking for prey. A thin stream of saliva ran from its mouth. It walked a few more paces, then stopped, swinging its head from side to side, like a bull waiting to charge.

Its fingers began scrabbling at the cave walls, peeling off chunks of moss. It sniffed at the green chunks, then began chewing on them. A few moments later it spat the moss out. It began overturning the rocks, looking for more to eat.

Slowly, cautiously, Endril pulled an arrow from his quiver. At the same time, Cal began drawing his sword. There was a slight, scraping sound as metal moved against metal. The Cyclops tossed its head up, eye wide, nostrils flared. It was alert for any movement.

All of them froze, afraid even of the sounds their hearts made pounding in their chests.

The beast went back to foraging under the rocks for food. It found some slugs, pale white in the gloom, and squatting on its haunches, began picking them off and eating them. It made contented, slobbering sounds. Bith shut her eyes. Cal felt his gorge rising. Hathor turned away.

Endril fitted the arrow to the bow. He was hoping the animal would simply leave. He did not want to fight this monstrosity. He wondered if it were an illusion conjured up by Schlein, but it hardly seemed to matter. The thing had substance, and whether it had been bred on this earth or was a madman's nightmare seemed of little importance now.

The creature rose and began shuffling toward them. It paused again to sniff the air, and a growl came from its throat. Its eye swiveled and stared in their direction.

"Go away . . . go away . . . go away," Bith said to herself, over and over, in a desperate chant.

It took a gigantic step forward, toward them. Abruptly, Endril got to his feet, arrow cocked. The Cyclops roared and swiped at him. The arrow shot forward and hit the animal's eye. There was a sickening sound of something soft exploding, and the creature screamed. Then, suddenly, it vanished. There was nothing there. The cavern still echoed with the Cyclop's cries.

Trembling, they came out of hiding. "Good shot, Endril," Cal said, trying to make light of what happened. He forced a smile.

"Another of Schlein's illusions," Endril said, "but it was real . . . it was flesh and blood . . . I'm certain."

Bith said, "Vili told us that as the sorcerer gained in skill, the dreams would become real. It would seem that Schlein has been applying himself." She too tried to smile, but the others could see that she was deadly pale and trembling. Cal reached out to her, but she stepped back a pace.

"I'm fine," she said. "This isn't anywhere near as bad as those initiation tests Meg told us about. How can I expect to ever become a great sorceress if I'm afraid of a dumb brute? Let's move on. We must get the Dreamstone from Schlein."

They walked until they were sure there would never be an end to it. They were weary and thirsty. Although dozens of side passages came into view, there always seemed to be a main route that led ever deeper into the mountain. They stayed on this path, never leaving it, too exhausted to wonder what they would reach at its end.

Finally, they came to another large chamber. Someone had been there before them. There was a table and a chair. On the table was an unlit candle, burned halfway down, and some sort of bound volume.

The air here was very cold, and they could see the clouds their breath made. Soon all of them were shivering.

Endril reached into his pack and found his tinderbox. He held the flint and steel against the candle wick and struck them until they sparked. The wick caught, and the candle's flame cast a small, unsteady light in the cave. It was reflected in the stalactites hanging from the ceiling, and tiny points of flame seemed to illumine the room.

Bith opened the book, fumbling with the thick parchment leaves. Her fingers felt stiff from cold. She saw that the pages were filled with a flowing script—it was a journal.

Cal peered over her shoulder. "What is it?"

"I think it's Schlein's diary," she said in a hushed voice. She scanned through the pages. "He chronicles his study of the Dreamstone."

"Read it to us," Endril said. "What is recorded there may be to our profit."

"Anything for a rest," Cal added.

Bith sat down in the chair and began to read.

Day 1

I begin this journal in a mood of elation and fear. My master has granted to me a gift, a sign of his favor— an amulet of great power. Last night, he came to me in my chamber. I thought I slept, but he was too real. I saw him as a column of mist and flame, and his voice was made of wind and ash.

He gave me this crystal he calls the Dreamstone, and it is a thing of beauty and wonder. It glittered in my hand with the cold light of a diamond, but its light was shot through with red fire.

It hangs from a silver chain which he has forged, and as I hung it about my neck, I was seared by the heat that came from it. When I awoke this morning, my first thought was that I had dreamt, but the stone is here—solid and tangible.

With this stone, I shall control the minds of men and women, and shape shadows so that they walk in this world as though they were born of this earth. My creatures shall populate the land.

Day 2

I must learn to master the Dreamstone. Within it is imprisoned a demon, and I shall bend it to my will. I am weary, for I wrestled with the thing all last night, trying to control it. It is fierce, but I believe I felt it yield to me, at least in part.

At dawn, I finally slept, but the stone haunts me, even now. I feel the hot eye of the demon upon me. I live constantly within an inferno. But my suffering shall not be in vain. Once I have mastered the stone, I shall cast my vengeance on those who have defied me. Revenge will be sweet and slow.

Day 3

I have made some progress. Last night I ordered a soldier brought to me. I bade him sleep in my chamber, telling him that I was ill and wanted someone near at hand to fetch water and food for me if I needed it.

He was a poor, simple creature. I watched him as he slept—the steady, slow breathing, the flickering of the eyelids, the occasional snore. He and all his kind are so vulnerable, so pathetic.

I resolved to wring that quietude from him. I struggled for control of the stone, and, gradually, achieved my aim. I envisioned evil dreams, such as those that would strike at the heart of any ordinary man. I gave him dreams of sickness, death, and grief.

His crude mind lay open to me—I saw old memories of a hated, brutal father and made him live again. I saw the death of a younger sister—and her death was made real to him.

He sweated and groaned in his sleep. I saw tears course down his face. But I grew weak. The concentration and will that is required to control the stone, even for such a simple task, is enormous. He broke from my grasp and awoke. So great was his terror, his eyes started from his head. I'm certain that, had my strength been greater, I could have killed him.

I was gentle with him, as he scrambled from his bed—all solicitation and concern. I sent him from me, telling him to look to his own health. Today I saw him going about his duties—his face was drawn and troubled. Last night will live long with him.

Bith put the book down. "I do not wish to read anymore. The words are too foul for me to hear them in my own voice." Endril took the journal from her. "I will read."

Day 4

I am very tired, but it is a tiredness that follows exultation, not the commonplace weariness that besets those lesser than myself. My growing power rends and tears at me.

Awake, I feel the stone hot against my chest, and its image burning into my brain. Asleep, I feel the demon scrabbling at me with its claws, and wake again with shadowy memories of a column of mist and fire, of laughter like burning ash.

Does my master come to me in my sleep and aid me in my struggle? Perhaps it is so. I shall take his strength and make it my own. Who knows what may come of this? I have thoughts I dare not put on paper. They shall remain hidden, for now.

I do not regret anything.

Day 7

It is several days since I have written, for I have taken a retinue, and moved to these caverns far beneath the earth. It is easier to find seclusion here, away from the intrusions of others. I have no time to spare from my great work.

Privacy is not difficult to come by. My servants scurry from me like mice from the cat. They sense my power and they fear me. All of them suffer from evil dreams. They whisper to each other in these echoing caverns, sharing their petty fears.

I seem stalled in my progress with the stone. I have done much, but a great deal of its power remains untapped. It whispers to me and taunts me. I am never free of it.

Day 10

Last night, after days of struggle, another triumph. After many hours of intense concentration, I saw a shape gather itself out of nothingness. It wavered and then solidified into the image I had in my mind—a serpent. It lay coiled at my feet, and, as I moved, followed me with its cold eyes. In my astonishment, my concentration wavered, and the creature vanished. But, in the dirt, was the imprint of its body.

Day 12

I have seen no one today. My thoughts occupy me completely. Odd visions come to me—I see ruined castles, and in my mind, walk through their once stately halls, hearing only the echoes of my own footsteps.

I see ancient burial places, with tombs of great magnificence, but all crumbling away before the steady assault of time.

My visions all speak of decay and loss. Soon I shall

be beyond these things. I shall be immutable, un-changeable. I have moved to another chamber, far from all the others. Their thoughts, buzzing about my head like a swarm of gnats, is too distracting. Also, the clutter of my room, filled with foolish objects, pains me.

I am being pared to the bone, to my essential self. I shed each useless skin with fierce joy. I discard all useless ties, all tawdry pastimes. My body reflects the state of my spirit. My flesh, with its desires and needs, burns away like all else that is foolish.

I feel a presence beside me—is it the demon of the stone? Is it my master? I cannot tell. It whispers to me, telling me secrets.

Perhaps the whisperer is myself? What does it mat-ter? The voice speaks of loneliness, of desolation, of glory. The loneliness is that of kings, the desolation of those who walk in the cold, bare places which lesser beings cannot stand.

I weary of this journal. Words do not matter. They are for the rest of humanity that chatters like a pack of monkeys. Power inconceivable is mine. I am ele-vated beyond all others.

There is nothing more to say.

Endril shut the book. "There is no more written."

All of them were silent for a moment, shaken by what he had read.

"He is mad," Cal whispered.

"He has made more progress since this last entry," Bith said thoughtfully. "His power has grown."

"He's a deluded fool," Endril said. "He's being used as some sort of intermediary by the Dark Lord. I'm certain that's what happening. As surely as Schlein manipulated the soldier, so the Dark Lord uses him. Schlein is too obsessed to see it.''

"Meg said the Dark Lord used the stone to control his followers. Perhaps this is one way he did it," Bith replied.

"Shall we go on?" Endril asked. "We must get that stone."

"I am more resolved than ever," Bith said.

"How admirable!"

They turned. Schlein was standing there, his arms folded across his chest. His body had wasted away, and his eyes burned in his skull-like face. He looked like a man being devoured by a fever.

Cal's sword was out. "You pompous fool, I've a few scores to settle with you, no matter what happens to me."

Schlein smiled and snapped his fingers. Armed men came from out of the side passages. Their weapons were drawn.

"Spare me your heroics, Caltus," Schlein said. "Watch this young idiot," he told his men. "He's extremely anxious to die. I wish to defer that event for a little while. Take his sword."

Cal stiffened. He was determined to fight rather than surrender his weapon, but Endril intervened. "Give them the sword, Cal. Don't throw your life away. We're not beaten yet."

"I never knew elves to be such optimists, Master Endril," Schlein said. "Their minds always seemed tinged with melancholy. Perhaps your human acquaintances are influencing you. Very instructive, I'm sure."

A soldier took Cal's sword and, with a stiff bow, offered it to Schlein. The wizard took it and examined it closely. "An interesting weapon. The runes bear close study. I will peruse them at my leisure. I don't think you will be needing it any time soon.

"Did you enjoy my little entertainment, my friends—the

Cyclops? My pet was quite real, was it not? It was mere show, of course. One might call it an elementary demonstration. I wanted to impress you. I can do much, much more.''

He turned to Endril. ''You are an excellent marksman, sir. I rather thought my creation would have you, but it was not to be.

''I have many such creatures inhabiting these caverns now. Perhaps I will introduce you to some of them. You are all such brave warriors. I'm sure Caltus, for instance, would enjoy battling them.

''And Bith, my dear,'' he said, turning to her, ''you are more beautiful than ever. How like your mother you grow. I hope you believe me when I assure you that I bear no grudge because you rejected my suit. All that is quite behind me now. I have other interests.''

''Then why would you send that vision?'' Bith asked. She tried to sound haughty and scornful. It never did to show fear before a bully like Schlein. ''Were you not trying to make me come to you, yet again?'' She laughed. She wondered if anyone else could see the crystal that hung about his neck.

Schlein's face twitched. ''Softly, my lady. Perhaps the vision *was* an error on my part.'' He smiled again, as if to show how graciously he could admit to error. ''That old witch still has some power. I underestimated her.

''I suppose you went to her for help, Master Endril? A waste of time, I assure you. You thought you would see the sorceress of your people's legends. But the world has changed much since those days. Her star is waning. Ours is waxing. The elves always were a nostalgic people. Sentimentality is such a weakness in these difficult times, don't you agree?

''Still, it has worked out for the best. After all, you are

here, including my lovely, charming Elizebith. It is as I intended.''

Schlein laughed. ''All of you have been nuisances. That time is ended. I think I'll have you killed—slowly, in a special way. I shall make your fears and dreams my special study. You have had just a taste of what I can do. But none of you understand how great my power has become. I must do something to correct that.''

''You are a dupe and a fool,'' Elizebith said. ''The Dark Lord uses you as a pawn in his game, and you think you make the moves yourself. He destroys you, uses your will and your determination to control the Dreamstone, and all the while you think you are becoming a rival to your master.''

Bith laughed again. ''You are his puppet—nothing more. He stays safely in the background and lets his lackey do his work.''

''So you know of the stone, do you?'' Schlein ran the pommel of Cal's sword along the side of her face and smiled again when she jerked away.

''You have been diligent in your research. Do you know that it is calling all the Dark Lord's servants to him? Your mother is among them. It would be interesting to keep you alive until she arrives. It sounds quite touching.

''Besides, you underestimate me. I tell you I am no servant, no mindless lackey. I am greater than you can imagine, and someday, someday soon, I may even challenge the Dark Lord and usurp him. I was not born to be anyone's servant. The fulfillment of my destiny is close.'' His voice rose and his eyes looked wild.

''Have I not labored to control the demon? It is I who manage it, not the Dark Lord. He grows slack and lazy while I grow in knowledge and power.'' He stopped abruptly, obviously trying to control himself. His next words were low and calm.

"But, you are so silent, Elizebith. You were always one for words. Surely you have something witty and clever to say? I am interested in your thoughts. Share them with me."

"I do nothing at your bidding," Bith said. "You weary me with your bragging and boasting."

She tried not to stare at the stone. Schlein didn't seem to realize she could see it, and that was to her advantage. It was difficult, though. Its allure was hypnotic and she longed to stare into it, to touch it. The facets caught the little light that was in the cavern and magnified it until the stone was as brilliant as a single star in the night sky.

Bith forced herself to keep her eyes on Schlein's face and her hands at her sides. She wondered if she would be able to snap the chain by herself. If the Dark Lord himself had forged it, she doubted that any spell she could conjure, unaided, would be strong enough.

As these difficulties presented themselves to her, her heart sank. Schlein would never take the Dreamstone off voluntarily—she was certain of that. Inwardly, she cursed Meg. Where was a legendary sorceress when you needed her? Compared to Schlein, Bith knew herself to be green as grass. She could never overpower him with her magic.

"You always were a contrary little thing, Elizebith," Schlein said. "So like your mother, you know. She too is willful. But she will be brought to heel, as will you, and your companions.

"Take them to the upper chamber," he ordered. "Make sure they are well secured, especially the troll. He is the strongest."

"Halt, villain!" The voice boomed, echoing and re-echoing in the cavern.

Schlein whirled around. "Who . . ."

Reflected in the stalactites, in the pools of water that lay on the floor, and even in the metal candleholder, was a face. It was a male face, bearded, and its blue eyes blazed with fury. The bushy eyebrows formed a single line across the top of the nose and the lines of the forehead were as taut as drawn wires.

Vili? Bith thought in astonishment.

"You follow the traitor?" Vili boomed. "He dares challenge me? Am I not the Dark Lord? And you, you fools, you lackwits, you obey the orders of this charlatan? You will be punished if you do not release them. Stand away, I say!"

"Who . . . " Schlein gaped. "Is this a joke?" His men, totally bewildered, stared at the images reflected over and over again.

"You fools!" Schlein roared. "Are you so dazzled by this paltry trick?"

And then, everything happened at once.

Schlein shouted something in a strange, gutteral tongue.

The stalactites began shattering, exploding into thousands of fragments. The face disappeared.

Cal snatched his sword away and began swinging.

Schlein's men, terrified, bolted into the passages.

Schlein reached out for Bith.

Bith heard Meg's voice. "Get it now, get it now."

"Meg?" she said, turning and turning, trying to locate the voice.

She felt Schlein's hand on her shoulder, twisting her around to face him. His face was contorted in an ugly snarl.

"You little idiot," Meg said, "get it and get out of there. I can't keep this up forever."

Bith's arm shot forward. Her hand clasped the chain around Schlein's neck. She felt a surge of power run down her arm.

This isn't me, this isn't my doing, she thought. She yanked on the chain. It snapped in her hand, and that small sound echoed in her ear more loudly than all the shouting that surrounded her.

Schlein's hands shot up and clasped his temples. He screamed over and over.

"Run, run." Meg's voice came to her again.

Bith ran.

CHAPTER 9

"Bith, come back," Cal shouted. He was looking in her direction, trying to figure out a way to get to her when he saw her make a headlong dash into the caverns.

"Seize them, seize them," Schlein shouted. His face was livid. "The false demon is gone—I have conquered him. Take them or suffer the consequences. And you"—he jabbed his finger at a clump of soldiers—"bring back that girl."

But Vili wasn't beaten yet. Reflected in the thousands of fragments were thousands of tiny faces, each with its own voice, telling the men to desert, to run.

"I am not beaten. I am like the Hydra—now I have many faces instead of one. I am everywhere you turn, and you can no more escape me than you can escape the air surrounding you."

Seeing his chance, Cal whirled on the soldiers and began battling his way back to Endril and Hathor. His two friends had managed to sidle toward an entrance during the confusion created by Vili's trick. Cal could see Hathor's axe rising and falling with clockwork regularity.

Schlein's men were frightened and confused. The ap-

125

paritions terrified them, and they were uncertain of what they were seeing or what to believe. Some of them took advantage of the confusion and bolted. They gave no thought to what would happen once they had run. All they knew was that this place was too terrible. Even Schlein's wrath was better than battling demons.

"Caltus, to us, to us," Endril called.

"Out of the way, my friend," Cal shouted to a rather bemused-looking soldier. He gave him a shove and sent the man flying into three others. They fell over into a heap.

"Bith ran that way," Cal shouted to Endril, pointing in the direction he had seen Bith take. "We have to get her." He saw Hathor pick up a soldier and hurl him across the chamber.

The man's flight was frightening and funny at the same time. His expression was utterly blank, as though hurtling through the air was only an ordinary duty in an ordinary day. For a moment, Cal doubted it was really a man, so natural did his flight seem.

But he did come to rest. It was the heavy, clumsy sound of his falling that caused his companions to spin around and look at him. He wasn't hurt by his fall, but he was almost killed in the stampede of Schlein's men fleeing from what they now were certain were demons.

The chamber was empty of soldiers as suddenly as it had been filled with them. Hathor's axe hung in the air, arrested in mid-swing. "Where everybody go?" he asked. He sounded irritated. "Wanted to fight more."

"Bravo, my heroes. Well-fought." It was Vili, still present in the chamber. Instead of the strident, booming voice he had used before, he spoke in whispers. "I can do no more for you now. My power is almost exhausted. I cannot remain in this sphere. Bith has gone to fulfill her quest. You must help her. Farewell, farewell. We shall meet again."

The images stuttered and flickered, like candle flames in a strong wind. Faintly, they heard the words, "I was magnificent, was I not?" and then there was nothing.

"Wait, come back," Endril cried. But only silence answered him. "So much is still unanswered," he said. "Where is Schlein, and what has happened to Bith?" They listened to the sound of water dripping down the walls. Endril stamped his foot in exasperation.

"We can't dally here," Cal said. "Vili's gone. Schlein's run off someplace to lick his wounds. We must go after Bith while we have the chance. We can't let her wander through these tunnels alone. You know what happened in her dream—it's dangerous for her to be by herself. Why did she run off that way? It isn't like her at all."

Endril shook his head. "I do not know. But I wonder if it could be because of the Dreamstone."

"I didn't see any stone," Cal said. "Do you think she went off to look for it? She should have waited."

"Do you remember what Meg said?" Endril responded. "Very few people can see it. We know it is usually worn on a chain around the neck. From Schlein's diary, I cannot believe he would ever be without it. Perhaps Bith saw it and somehow managed to take it from him. I don't know how she could get it from Schlein, but it's all that makes sense."

"Then we know what she looks for," Hathor said. "Waterfall."

"Let's go," Cal said.

Schlein sat in a corner, his head in his hands. He was weeping. "Lost, lost, how could it be lost? I must get it back. The little bitch, the thief. She thinks she'll learn how to use it and she will rule. I know her thoughts. But she cannot. It is mine, I have made it mine. It will heed no other."

His head throbbed, and he pressed his hands to his temples, trying to stop the pain. He knew that when the stone was torn from him it left a raw, gaping wound within his mind. Invisible to normal sight, it was real nonetheless. A stroke of pain made him writhe in agony.

He staggered to his feet, using the wall for support. Sweat dripped from his forehead. The room swam before him, then gradually steadied.

This room had been his chamber until he had gone further beneath the earth in his search for solitude. He noted the hastily built shelves, burdened with books, bottles, and the tools of his art. He had hoped to leave all this behind, to need none of it to work his magic. The Dreamstone was more powerful than everything else he possessed.

"But I will use the lesser as my stepping stone to the greater," he murdered. "I still have much power at my command. There are spirits who are sworn to do my will.

"They are clever, those four. This has been their goal all along—to steal the stone and use it for their own. They think to overthrow the Dark Lord and become the new masters. All of this has been a plot. She made me lust after her, she used me. They think they have triumphed, but I shall foil them. They are fools to think they can beat me.

"They forget that she is little more than a child," he said, continuing to talk to himself. "She cannot master the stone at once. She may be unable to master it at all. It takes a highly accomplished sorcerer to wield it. I will find her shortly—they will pay for this." He began assembling an odd collection of chalk, candles, and small bones. Then, slowly, with a piece of chalk, he drew an intricate diagram on the floor—a spiral enclosing a square. The narrowest part of the spiral touched, but did not cross, the square.

At each corner of the square, he placed a candle. He then inscribed characters along the square's borders. At the widest portion of the spiral he put the bones. Then, from another shelf he took a brazier and a stand. He set them at the spiral's narrowest point.

Stepping just outside of the square, he placed some small pieces of wood in the brazier and lit it. A smell of sandlewood and spices filled the chamber.

"I will get it back," he said, muttering through clenched teeth. "I am not beaten." He drew a small dagger from his belt. The tip glinted like a shark's tooth.

He rolled up the sleeve of his robe and dragged the knife point down the inside of his upper arm. There was pain, but compared to the pain from his hidden wound the slash in his arm was no more than a pinprick. With an expression of complete indifference, he watched the blood seep from the wound.

"I have conquered chaos and the pit," he intoned softly. "I have braved the trials of my clan and triumphed. I have dared the three levels and the seven tiers, and I exist at the source. I stand at the fount of disorder and the wellspring of grief. You who dwell at the heart of despair, appear, appear, appear." He clapped his hands together.

The flame in the brazier flared upward and the temperature of the room plummeted. Schlein began to tremble in the cutting cold. He heard his heart slamming like a latchless door in the wind. The atmosphere of the room was taut, explosive. But nothing else happened.

"Do not trifle with me," he rasped. He pointed at the flame, and somewhere a dog began to howl. The sound grew in volume until the bottles on the shelves rattled.

"What wouldst thou?" a voice said. It was deep and hollow, and sounded like wind whipping through trees. "Why do you disturb my rest?"

"Appear, as I commanded you. I demand obedience."Schlein jabbed the small knife into the flame. The howling began again.

The smoke rising from the brazier began to writhe, its plumes thickening and drawing together. The walls of the room thrummed and vibrated, like a great heart. There was a terrible stench, as of something that lay rotting in murky water. Then there was a clap of thunder, and the room grew dark. The flickering candles could be seen like lamps in a heavy fog.

A shape appeared in the square. It grew and coalesced into a large grey wolf that stared at Schlein with unblinking yellow eyes.

"Transform, I say," Schlein hissed. "Show thy true self, or I shall keep thee imprisoned here all the days of my life." He put the knife into the fire again, and the wolf threw back its head and howled. It disappeared with a popping sound.

There was a heavy silence, and the smoke again began dipping and swirling. A naked man appeared in the square. He was powerfully built and handsome. His long hair was made of flames that twisted about him ceaselessly like a nest of serpents. But he had the same eyes as the wolf.

"Speak, sorcerer," the demon said. "Why dost thou trouble me with thy foolish demands?"

"Thou knowest full well my mind. I have lost that which is precious to me," Schlein said. "Recover it."

"I cannot."

"Why not? It is in the hands of a mere girl. Are you so weak you cannot wrest it from her?"

The demon looked at him with utter disdain. "You know that is not our way. I can tempt her to her ruin, to yield to the stone's powers, but I have not the power to pluck it from her hands. That is the way of mortals. Send out your guards and arrest her. Trouble me not. The coarse materiality of your world is not my concern.''

Schlein bit his lip. ''Tell me what you see,'' he commanded. The demon stared out. ''She is lost, and she is running. She wishes to rid herself of the stone, to lose it.''

''What!'' Schlein exploded. ''That cannot be. No one would deliberately lose such a powerful tool. You are lying. She means to make it her own. She thinks to set herself above us, as a queen. I know the way of demons. You would deceive me by telling me falsehoods.''

The demon smiled, revealing two long eyeteeth. ''You are too clever, my lord.'' It bowed.

Schlein eyed the demon warily. ''What of the others?'' he asked. ''What do they do?''

The demon shrugged. ''They search for the girl. They are concerned.''

''Can you do nothing for me?'' Schlein demanded angrily.

''Thou know full well what I can and cannot do. Thy time is short, magician, that is plain to me. Command me, or release me. I do not waste my time in idle gossip.''

''Then I command thee. Prey on their weaknesses, tempt them. Now, get thee gone.''

The demon snarled. ''Do not try to cheat me, sorcerer. Where is thy sacrifice, thy substitute?''

Schlein reached into a pocket of his robe and brought out a small stoppered vial. He tossed it across to the demon, who caught it in its mouth and swallowed it.

''It is acceptable for now, mage. But thou follow a narrow path, and thy steps are unsteady. I watch thy faltering and wait. Soon, soon, I shall have thee and I shall gnaw at thy mind till the end of time. The pain you feel now is but a foretaste of what is to come.''

''Do not threaten me, slave.'' Schlein thrust the knife

into the fire again. The demon howled and then, with another clap of thunder, it vanished.

Schlein walked unsteadily to a chair and collapsed. His face was ashen. "Guard!" he called out.

"Sir." An armed soldier came into the room, bowing.

"Get me Targ."

"Yes, sir."

Schlein tried to get control of himself again. It did not do to look anything but composed in front of the orc captain. He was more than half a brute.

"Captain Targ, reporting."

The orc shuffled in, with the half-stooping walk of his kind. Tall and broad, with wide shoulders and long muscular arms, he was a formidable fighter, as those who had challenged him for his captaincy would have attested—if they had still been alive to do so.

Along with his prowess as a fighter, he was cunning and bold. He enjoyed his work. Schlein found him invaluable and made sure he was well paid and that the choicest loot of any raiding party was his.

"Targ, be seated." Schlein gestured to a chair. It creaked under the orc's bulk.

"My men have failed me, Targ," Schlein began. The orc grunted, as if to say he was not surprised.

"They have allowed important captives to escape—one of them with some extremely valuable property. They are a pack of superstitious, gullible cowards."

"Hah, these are things I know and I tell you," Targ said. "My troops, they are all these things too, but they know if they don't obey or make bad mistake, I hunt them down and kill them. Discipline very important for good army."

Schlein smiled. "You are my best leader. I can always rely on you. The ones I search for are loose in the tunnels—an elf, a young man, a troll, and a young woman. I want the girl alive—the others . . . '' Schlein shrugged, to show his indifference. ''Their bodies will do . . . but I want no meddling with them—understand?''

Targ got up. ''I understand. There is, of course, a reward for their capture . . . ?''

''A lavish reward, Captain, I assure you.''

Targ rose from his seat. ''Then I must make haste. We will comb the tunnels. Never fear, they will be found.''

Schlein gave him what little information he had about the prisoners' escape and dismissed him. After Targ had left, Schlein sat brooding in front of the fire. Now he could only wait.

Targ went down to the caverns where his troops were quartered. It was a minimal complement. Schlein had not come here to fight battles.

He didn't enter right away. Instead, he stayed back in the shadows. His keen sight let him see into the fire-lit cavern, and he could easily hear what was being said. Orcs were not known for their gentle voices and subdued tones. He always liked to know what his troops were doing and saying in his absence.

The orcs were in their filthy quarters, sprawled around a cooking fire. A piece of meat was roasting on a spit. Whenever one of them felt hungry, he would reach over and tear off a strip, gulping it down before one of his fellows snatched it from him.

''He's losing his grip, if you ask me,'' said Garik, a small grey orc with red eyes.

''He's lost something,'' said his companion, Kang. ''His brains.'' Garik squealed with laughter at his friend's joke.

''Weeping and holding his head . . . I saw him,'' Kang continued. ''He's come to the end of his tether, if you ask me. There's been too many foul-ups lately. Have you seen what he looks like? Bones that decided to get up and go for a walk. And he's always looking over his shoulder, as if he's afraid of something stalking him. Not only that, but they say a demon sent all his men-troops running.

"Men!" Kang went on, his voice heavy with contempt. He spat. "I hate them—with their faces like sheep and puny bodies. Why do we follow them? It is orcs who do the fighting, orcs who do the killing. Yet it is always we who get the leavings. The men run from their own shadows, crying for their mothers, yet always they get the best."

Garik nodded his agreement. "Aye, we should rebel. We could cut them all down like the wheat in the fields."

He reached for the sizzling meat and dug his claws into the joint's side. He ripped off a piece, clouting another orc in the ear to keep him from taking it.

"Give it to me," Kang demanded. "I want it."

"Get a piece yourself. You're a greedy, lazy pig if you ask me."

"I didn't ask you," Kang snarled. He hurled himself at Garik, and they rolled over and over on the floor.

"Fight, fight," the other orcs screamed in unison. They hastily scrambled to their feet and formed a ring around the two who were scuffling and snarling.

"I bet on the bigger one."

"I say we eat the loser."

"I say you break this up," said Targ, striding into the room. He bared his long yellow fangs. The other orcs stepped back a pace.

Targ pushed through to where Kang and Garik were fighting. Kang was on top, biting at Garik's ear. Targ reached down and picked Kang up by the throat. He hurled him away as easily as if he were tossing a ball. Garik's eyes widened when he saw Targ, and he scrambled away.

"Get your gear together," Targ ordered. "We've a job

to do. As usual, it's left to us orcs to clean up the mess the men leave. But, if we succeed, there'll be a great reward. There's escaped prisoners to find—a man, a troll, an elf, and a woman.

"Try to take them all alive, but especially the girl. She's the really important one. Any harm comes to her, and you'll pay. But don't let me catch any of you looting the bodies of the others, or you'll have me to deal with on that score too!

"We'll split up into groups to search the tunnels. I'll take you to where they were last seen—the lower chamber Schlein's been using. We also know what direction the girl ran, so she might not be too hard to find. I'll assign you individual areas when we're at the chamber. And I'm leading the pack that hunts down this girl.

"On this job, use your noses. They'll help you more than eyes. You all know the stink of human, elf, and troll. Are there any questions?"

The orcs were silent. Targ nodded. "Good. Follow me. We will get them. Then there will be fun."

CHAPTER
10

Bith ran blindly, never looking back, never stopping. Panic blurred her vision, made her heart slam against her ribs, and, with its whiplash, drove her ever deeper into the mountain.

She felt the Dreamstone bumping against her breast, warming her with its heat. Then her foot tripped over a rock and she went sprawling.

Feeling her balance go, she gathered the silver chain tightly in her hand, lest she lose it in the fall. She hit the ground hard. The shock knocked the breath from her body. Stunned, unable to move, she lay there, clutching the Dreamstone to her.

The temptation to look at it was overwhelming. Hesitantly, she held the crystal up and examined it. Even in the murk of the caverns, it glowed with an intense light. She peered more closely. In each of its many facets there seemed to be a figure dancing. But she couldn't be sure. They were obscured, veiled, as if layers of gossamer lay between her world and theirs.

Worlds within worlds were captured inside the Dreamstone. She remembered, as a child, seeing an odd painting of a room. In that room was a painting of the same room, and that room held again the duplicate of itself.

She had pondered over this mystery, in her childish way, long and hard. More than anything she had wanted to find the last room—or would it be the first?—the source from which all the other rooms sprang.

The Dreamstone presented a like riddle. But she was an adult now, with reason and power on her side. Surely she could penetrate to the center and find the beginning. What secrets lay hidden there?

As she bent her head yet closer to the stone, there was a sudden, sucking sound, and she felt as if she were being pulled into the crystal. Abruptly, she jerked away and let go of the chain. The Dreamstone again rested upon her breast. Was it her imagination, or did it burn hotter than before?

"Come to your senses," she told herself fiercely. "Meg told you to let it alone. It's dangerous, seductive. You almost fell into its trap. Your duty is to dispose of the thing, and that's what you're going to do. So, on your feet, missy, as Meg would say, and get on with your business!"

Standing was easier said than done. As soon as she put her weight on her left foot, pain shot through her ankle, making her gasp. Gingerly, she bent over and tried to examine it. The ankle seemed to be swollen. Massaging the tender skin made her wince with pain.

She gritted her teeth and began to walk. It was little more than a hobble. The urge to break down and cry was very strong. Loneliness gnawed at her. Fear for herself and for her friends preyed on her mind. What had happened to Cal, Hathor, and Endril? Would they think she had deserted them, fled out of cowardice, leaving them to the enemy? A wave of shame washed over her.

"I should have stayed," she told herself. "They won't

know what happened to me, or why I did what I did. *I* don't even know why I did it. Following voices . . . what's gotten into me?''

The emptiness of the caverns preyed on her. It was like being entombed. Any sign of another living thing would have been welcome. But there was only the sound of her own stumbling footsteps on the hard rock.

Tired and hungry, she concentrated grimly on her task. It took conscious effort to keep putting one foot in front of the other.

What difference would it make if I simply sat here for the rest of my life, she thought wearily. *Let whatever happens, happen. Walk in the cold, walk in the dark and what for? I'm tired and I'm scared. I don't care what happens anymore.*

But, stubbornly, she kept going. ''Try to think of something more cheerful,'' she said to herself. Her mind remained a blank. ''Bith, Bith, there's all sorts of good news. First, you're not dead—not yet anyway. Second, you haven't been captured by Schlein. You don't have to listen to his raving, or his marriage proposals for that matter. Third, you've gotten the Dreamstone away from him. And, best of all, think how miserable he must feel!'' At this, her mood lightened somewhat, but it was only for a moment.

''I wonder where the others are?'' Her mood plummeted again. Tears welled in her eyes. ''Surely, they can't be captured. They can outthink and outfight Schlein blindfolded and one-legged. I'm certain they're looking for me. It's so awful being alone. There's no trouble so bad that being alone doesn't make it worse. In my dream I was alone, and I died.''

Struck by a sudden thought, she stopped and fumbled in her pouch. Finally, she found what she was looking for—

a bit of chalk. "Foolish girl," she whispered. "Why didn't you think of this before?"

Carefully, she tried to write on the cavern wall. The walls were slick and wet, the chalk little more than a nubbin, but before it completely crumbled in her hand, she managed to inscribe a large, ragged *B* on the rock, and a smaller arrow showing her direction.

She stood back and surveyed her work. It was barely visible in the dim light, and she feared that the chalk would be washed away, but it was the best she could do. Any effort was better than none.

The thought struck her that others besides her friends would be looking for her. This sign might as soon bring her enemies as anyone. Still, it was a risk she was prepared to take. Just the act of leaving some evidence of her passing was comforting. Let her mark stand for her defiance and courage as well as her need.

As she stood there, Bith realized she was shivering. A chill wind was blowing, but she couldn't tell from where. It had sprung up suddenly, with no forewarning.

She started to shudder. "It's cold, so cold. I hate being cold. It wasn't this bad a moment ago." The throbbing pain in her ankle seemed worse, and she leaned against a rock to take her weight off it.

A faint, malodorous smell came to her. That, and the freezing air, made her feel nauseous. Irresistibly, the thought came to her that her friends were dead, that all effort was useless. Despair washed over her.

Her mind was filled with pictures—simple, explicit, and terrifying. Private horrors she had voiced to no one paraded before her eyes, impossible to deny. And always there was the cold that bit deeper than any knife. It immobilized her, turning her body to an icy statue.

The only spot of warmth was the stone that lay, hot as a living thing, against her body.

Her hand crept up to the chain, like a creature separate from her, with a will of its own. It hungered for heat the way a starving animal hungers for food. No risk was too great. She clasped the stone and gazed into it.

"I'll only look for a moment," she told herself. "Just to warm up a bit. There's no harm in that." The light from the Dreamstone was dazzling, and now it reminded her of a burning ember. It must be warm at the heart of the crystal. An inner prompting too strong to resist riveted her eyes to the stone.

Again, the figures danced before her. They were clearer than before. Graceful as saplings, they bent and twisted before her, their arms interlaced, linking facet to facet. There was that same strange smell in the air, sweet now, but with an underlying bitterness. She felt sleepy, dreamy. The figures came together, melting, the boundaries of one blending into those of the others.

The light engulfed her, washing over her like warm water. The world took on an unreal, reddish tinge. She was a mermaid, at home in strange seas, swimming in light, moving toward the source that, like a beacon, drew her ever forward. It pulsated like a great, beating heart.

Another shape was forming, taking on definition. Eyes, penetrating, burning . . .

"Put it down, you little idiot!" The voice was harsh as a crow screaming in a field. Something shoved her hard, and she stumbled, landing on her bad ankle. The pain shattered her lethargy. Her return to the real world was as shocking and sudden as if she had been drowning and someone had suddenly yanked her from the water.

Startled out of her wits, she dropped the chain.

"Who's there?" she called. Her eyes were wide. "I heard

you, you meant me to hear you. I felt you, so why don't you show yourself? Meg? Cal? Is that you?'' No one answered. ''Caltus, if this is one of your moronic jokes, I swear, I'll turn you into something even your own mother couldn't love. Speak!''

''Speak!'' the caverns echoed back, as if to mock her. ''Speak, speak.''

Bith's shoulders sagged. *Maybe I only imagined it*, she thought. *I did seem to be dropping off.* She waited another moment, hoping to see someone. But she was still alone.

''Don't fret, Elizebith,'' she told herself sighing. ''You've a sprained ankle and you've gone mad. It could be worse. After all, sprained ankles heal, and you don't really need your wits. You never use them. Because, if you did, you wouldn't have gotten yourself into this fix in the first place! Now I know what a hero is—a fool! I can't wait to tell Cal.''

''We'll never find her,'' Cal groaned. ''She's lost in one place and we're lost in another. It's hopeless. How could I have let her get away from me? Her dream was a forewarning against letting her be by herself.''

They were baffled and confused, wandering endlessly through the tunnels. Cal had called Bith's name until he was hoarse. Endril, his hearing strained for the slightest sound, was also discouraged. What chance had they in this honeycomb of cold rock? This place was as like to be their tomb as anything else.

''You are not to blame,'' Endril said, laying a hand on Cal's shoulder. ''There was nothing to be done. Perhaps it is fate that we have been separated.''

He noticed that Cal had begun to shiver. The cavern seemed colder than before. Even Hathor, who was ordinarily oblivious to physical discomfort, was shaking. There was also an odd, unpleasant smell in the air.

Cal shrugged Endril off. He felt a spark of irritation that quickly flared into anger. *Does he never stop lecturing? He treats me like a child. Who is he to give advice? All of this is his fault*. The bitter thoughts buzzed around him like angry hornets. They pricked and spurred him on like goads.

"I am weary of words," Cal said aloud in an angry tone. "Elves are great talkers, great philosophers—a platitude for every occasion. They are enraptured with the sounds of their voices, and think that all should listen and obey."

His voice rose. "But I am a man of actions, not words. That is the difference between elf and human. Your people are lost in stories, songs, and sayings—all of them from a time long before even you were born.

"But we"—he pointed at his chest—"are concerned with the present, and the future. That is why your star is waning, while ours waxes strong and bright. Listening to you is listening to the past. What care I for the dead? That is what you are—a ghost, a sack of memories."

Endril's eyes narrowed. "Finally you speak what is in your black heart, Caltus. Then let me return the favor. I say that dealing with you humans has been distateful, disgusting. You are a shortsighted, vain, and violent people. Your little lives are over as quickly as a summer storm. You see nothing past your brief time here. Is it any wonder elves have long stayed aloof from your kind?

"Humans have done much to harm us. They cut down our trees, all of them with voices you are too deaf to hear. They kill without thought, and boast of it. They drown out all the other sounds in this world with their noise. Do not anger me beyond reason, Caltus Talienson, for there is a score to settle between elves and men."

Hathor hooted with laughter. "Funny, both of you." Cal

and Endril turned to look at him. "What are elves, what are humans, but fodder for trolls, eh?" Hathor laughed again, baring his yellow fangs.

"We are strongest. Men are small. Elves are skinny. Good for the pot. Fight you both." He took his axe and swung it around his head. "See who wins. Been too long—I like to fight. I forget how good it is to taste flesh."

The smell in the room thickened. It was charged with hostility. The three circled each other warily, like predators. Endril drew his dagger and Cal slowly unsheathed his sword. Then, an odd thing happened. A bluish tinge, so subtle at first that it might have been a trick of the light, crept along the length of the blade. The color intensified until the sword glowed bright blue.

"It is enchantment," Endril gasped.

"What does this mean?" Cal asked, his voice filled with wonder.

"We are bewitched," said Endril. "There is some demon here, some evil presence working its magic on us. The runes on this sword must be spells that warn of such things."

"I see no demon," Hathor said. He eyed Endril suspiciously. "Is trick."

"It is no trick," Endril said. "What have we been saying? Do the words of our mouths speak the truth in our hearts? We are being played with. Think! Fight this thing! It knows our fears, it knows the worst side of all of us, and it labors to bring it forth. Do not let it."

Cal and Hathor looked doubtful. Endril sheathed his dagger. "I make the first move. I defy this abomination."

He looked at his friends. He felt that all of them were teetering on the brink of destruction. Would the trust that had grown up between them prevail, or be swamped in the atmosphere of hatred that hovered in the room like a yellow fog?

Hathor dropped his axe. "I'll not be used. Things I say are things I have heard. But I say not true. I say no."

Tears welled in Cal's eyes. "What has come over us? I have never felt such hate. I was ready to do murder."

The blue glow of the sword began to fade. They felt the air become warmer, and the stench dissipated.

"Is gone?" asked Hathor.

"For now," Endril said. "I feel my mind once again belongs to me. But it will return, I'm certain."

Cal sheathed the blade. "Little did King Grimnison know the good he would do us when he gave me this. It has saved our lives—not by violence, but by stopping violence."

Endril nodded. "We must not forget the lesson we have learned. This sword may yet again save us from being led into evil. We are not done with this demon, I fear. It has been beaten, but barely. I fear it may return."

Cal forced a smile. "What would life be without challenges?"

Schlein stirred uneasily in his chair. He had dropped off to sleep, but his dreams were ugly. They were filled with an aching sense of loss and misery that made him groan and cry out as though he had been stabbed.

He remembered that he had dreamt of his master. The column of mist and fire had appeared before him, and it was beautiful and terrible in a way he could not describe. It gave off a light that, instead of revealing, seemed to cloak all in shadow. In perpetual unrest, it churned upon itself as waves do in a fierce storm. He prostrated himself before it. The column began to make an angry, surging sound.

He awoke suddenly, drenched in sweat, to a room that was still and dark. The fire had burned low. He filled a mug with wine from a pitcher on the table. His hands shook.

This is no good, he thought. *I must not lose my resolve or my strength.*

While he slept, someone had brought his supper, a platter of meat and a loaf of bread, leaving it on the table. No one disturbed Schlein if they could help it.

He tore off a chunk of bread, and forced down a few bites. The meat made his gorge rise and he shoved it away. He drank more wine, in great thirsty gulps.

Restlessly, he rose and paced the room, waiting for the news that would tell him of the Dreamstone's return. Pride and arrogance told him he could not fail, but some deeper fear whispered that the stone was lost.

He tensed. He sensed the familiar chill, and his nostrils curled at the rank smell. Within the square he had drawn, a shape was forming, and then the demon stood there. Schlein furtively slipped the knife in his pocket back into his hand and approached. He studied it curiously. It looked, he thought—if the expression could rightly be applied to a demon—sulky.

"What hast thee to tell me?" Schlein asked.

"They are protected. Thou didst not say so. This is greater labor than our bargain specified."

"Protected? What do you mean?"

"The man has a sword covered in runes. It betrayed my presence. The one who carries the stone is watched over by another, who intruded upon my spell. None of this was told to me. I should have asked thee for much more."

"It was not told because it was not known."

The demon shrugged. "Thou art careless, old man. Thy power withers. Perhaps thy time is almost over. Thy master shall not be pleased when he learns that thou hast lost the Dreamstone." The demon smiled. It was not a pleasant sight.

Schlein winced. "I shall recover it. And I am not interested in excuses from thee, thou bumbler. Who watches over the woman?''

"I cannot tell. A mage, perhaps—but it is not certain. The presence is not always there. The power is, perhaps, not strong enough to be constant."

"That meddling old fool" Schlein muttered.

The demon laughed. "Thou art confounded, eh? Thou hast enemies stronger than thou, it would seem. Old man," the demon whispered, "come with me . . . " Suddenly, the demon snatched at Schlein.

He recoiled, and swiftly as a stinging adder, stabbed the small knife he had in his hand into the demon's arm. There was a sizzling sound, and the demon screamed.

Schlein pulled the knife out and stepped back. The blade was smoking. "I am still thy master, spirit. Do not forget it again." He drew himself up. "Remember me in thy hate as the one who has chastised thee; remember me in thy bitterness as one still great enough to chain thee. Be about thy duties, wretch. Do not fail me again."

"I shall remember thee well, Schlein." The demon's voice dripped with venom. It vanished.

Schlein fainted.

The orcs gathered around Targ in Schlein's underground tunnel. He sniffed the air and grinned. "The air stinks of them," he said. "The girl went down this passage." He jerked his thumb in the direction Bith had run.

"Search the other tunnels for a scent. If you find it, trail those other three. You know what's expected of you. Remember, don't meddle with the bodies. I will hunt down the woman."

Kang stepped forward. "Why you? Why must you always have the richest prize? Let some others search for her, too. Many others track as well as you."

"Because I say that is the way it will be!" He glared at Kang. "Do you object?"

Kang stepped back a pace. "No," he muttered. "I only asked."

"Good. Then get started."

Kang turned, as if to go back to the others. Then, with a bloodcurdling scream he pulled his long knife and leapt at Targ.

Targ sidestepped neatly. Clearly, he had not only been expecting an attack—he was hoping for one. As Kang's knife arced smoothly downwards, Targ grasped his wrist, arresting its murderous sweep.

They faced each other like clockwork figures whose gears have jammed—bodies frozen, arms quivering, as one sought to complete his movement and the other sought to arrest it.

Kang's arm began to shake as though he suffered from a palsy. His hand opened and the knife dropped to the ground. His breathing was strained, but he made no other sound.

Targ's other arm shot out, grasped Kang by the throat, and heaved him up off the ground. The sound of labored breathing stopped.

Kang's feet kicked frantically at first, then more slowly, then hung limp. Targ tightened his grip and there was a terrible, cracking sound. With a shout of triumph, Targ threw the body down. He glared at the other orcs.

"Any other questions?"

The orcs shook their heads.

"Good. Then be about your business. I will find the woman." Targ smiled.

CHAPTER
11

"Now what?" Cal said in disgust. "Do we turn back?" They had reached a dead end. The path they were following had dwindled to nothing and they were faced with a wall of mute stone.

"I hear water," Endril insisted.

"You've been saying that for half the day, or night, or whatever it is," Cal retorted. "I don't hear any water. And all I see is rock—and I'm sick of it."

Hathor looked around glumly. "Hungry," he muttered.

"Just don't start that again," Cal snapped.

"Look, up there . . . another entrance," Endril said. He pointed to a gaping hole high in the cavern wall.

Cal peered up. "You call that an entrance? For what? Eagles? Do you propose flying up there? I'm sorry, but I didn't bring my wings."

"You are so humorous, Caltus," Endril said. "I am certain the sound of water is from that direction. We must get up there."

"It's all very well, Endril, to say 'must,' but that begs the question of 'how.' I feel I'm skilled at many things, but I can't fly."

"You're beginning to sound like Bith," Endril grumbled. "I've a rope. If I can climb up there, I can lower the rope and haul you both up. It's no more than thirty feet."

"I can't tell you how reassured that makes me feel," said Cal.

"Can't do it. Afraid of heights," Hathor objected.

"Since when? You've never mentioned anything about that," Endril said. "We went over those mountains without your once being afraid."

"Didn't go through air," Hathor pointed out. "You go. I stay here and keep lookout. Lookout very important."

"I'm losing my patience with you two," Endril said. "I'm certain that if we can reach that cavern, we'll be close to the waterfall. Backtracking and searching for another route is risky and time-consuming. I intend to climb that wall. You can do what you like. Don't forget—Bith needs our help."

Resolutely, he dumped his pack on the ground and rummaged through it. He pulled out a coil of rope. "I never go anywhere without some rope," he said. "You can never tell when it will come in handy."

"Words for the wise . . . " Cal muttered.

Endril gave him an irritated look. Cal held up his hands in a gesture meant to placate. "I'll be quiet," he said.

"Good." Endril slipped the coil of rope over his shoulder. "Cal, bring my pack with you when I bring you up." He studied the wall intently, planning his way up. There were plenty of niches and handholds. He didn't think it would be too difficult. Still, he wished the wall was dryer.

Endril slipped one hand into a broad crack that ran across the rock. With the other, he grabbed a small protrusion jutting from the wall. He began to pull himself up.

Craning their necks, Hathor and Cal watched as the elf,

splayed spiderlike against the cavern wall, made his slow upward progress.

In a hushed voice, Cal said, "He's mad."

Hathor nodded.

"Only move one thing at a time," Endril reminded himself. "One hand . . . good . . . a foot . . . excellent . . . the other hand . . . now, the other foot." His foot found a niche and then slipped. He felt sick. Slowly, he prodded his boot into the wall, searching for another toehold. Finally, he found one. *Wonderful* he thought. *Another inch conquered.* He was terrified. *I hate heights.*

After what seemed like an eternity, he was at last eye level with the opening. He hauled himself up and lay there, panting. He wanted to kiss the ground.

"Endril," Cal called after him. "Are you all right?"

Endril peered out over the ledge. "Yes, quite, thanks. There's nothing to it." He smiled. "You're next, Cal." He let down one end of the rope.

"Tie it tight," he advised. "And hold on."

Cal looked up at him. "Don't worry." He turned to Hathor. "I have an idea. Why don't you go first? You're heavier. He'll run out of strength hauling me up."

Hathor handed him Endril's pack. "Don't forget this."

"Thanks, friend," Cal said, taking the pack and giving the troll a black look.

"Pleasure."

Cal wrapped the rope around his arm and held on for dear life. "All right, Endril—haul away. I'm ready to die."

Using his feet to push himself along, and with Endril pulling him up, Cal, feeling like a hooked fish, finally got to the top.

"You see," Endril said, "it's easy." He studied Cal carefully. "Are you feeling well? You look quite white."

"I'm fine," Cal answered, wiping the sweat from his face. He listened, his head cocked. "You know, I think you're right about the water."

"Of course I'm right," Endril answered.

He let down the rope again. "Hathor, get ready to come up. Cal hears the water, too."

"Oh, good." Hathor sounded distinctly unenthusiastic. Reluctantly, the troll tied the rope on and took a good grip. "Go."

Cal and Hathor hauled hard on the rope. "How heavy is he?" Cal gasped. Endril only shook his head. He didn't want to waste any breath. He gazed down at Hathor. The troll was simply hanging there limply. No wonder he felt like dead weight.

"Hathor," Endril shouted, "do something. Use your legs against the rock and your arms to pull yourself up. Give us some help. Don't hang there like a side of beef!"

Hathor up looked at him with a face of inconsolable woe. He kicked halfheartedly at the wall. "Want to go down," he said.

"You're an overgrown baby," Endril shouted again. He yanked on the rope.

"Overgrown is the word," Cal said under his breath.

Grunting and sweating, they hauled the unwilling Hathor up the wall and over the ledge. He got up slowly. After a moment he said, "Hear water. That way." He pointed down the tunnel.

"Thank you. We know," Cal said.

"Why wait, then? Have to find Bith." And with these parting words, Hathor marched resolutely down the tunnel.

"Can I kill him?" Cal asked.

"Wait until we're out of here," Endril replied.

They trailed after Hathor, talking softly to each other.

"This seems to join up into another tunnel," Endril observed.

"The whole place is a maze," Cal said. "Even if we find Bith and the waterfall, I don't see how we'll find our way out again. And another thing—Schlein must have sent people after us. I can't believe he's given up."

"One thing at a time," Endril said. "We still have many weapons at our command. We are not forgotten. Vili knows we are here, and, perhaps, Meg also. I do not believe they will desert us."

Cal laughed. "Vili's help has never been something to count on. And who knows about Meg? I've seen no sign of her."

"Bith may have. In any case, we are unharmed, and we have our wits about us. Schlein has never found us easy prey."

"I suppose not," Cal said glumly. "I only wish everything could be easier. Wouldn't it be lovely if we simply found the stone lying on a table, and we took it, dropped it into the nearest available river, and then went home? Why must everything be such a trial." He sighed.

Endril laughed. "What sort of hero are you? There'll be no more songs sung about the great Caltus Talienson if all your adventures are as tame as that."

"I suppose not," Cal answered. "But think how relaxing it would be! It's hard being a hero and a human being. In the stories, the heroes are heroes all the time. They're brave and fearless, and noble. It seems they're all of a piece.

"But I'm always a little of this and a little of that. I seem to be brave and frightened at the same time. I'll fight, but, to speak honestly, sometimes I wish I didn't have to. I wish I was anyplace else. I'll make a journey, but not without wishing for a soft bed and a good meal. It's all contradictions and contrariness. They never sing about that in the ballads.

"When I heard the song the Skrisung sang, about me, I didn't recognize myself." He laughed a little. "Brave, cunning, bold . . . " He shook his head. "In truth, I was so frightened, I wasn't even sure what I was doing. What kind of hero is that?"

"A real one," Endril said gently.

Abruptly, Hathor stopped. Cal, who hadn't been looking where he was going, walked right into him. "Hathor!" he exclaimed. "What ails you?"

"Look!" Hathor said, and pointed.

"What? Where?" Cal asked, drawing his sword. Then he saw.

Scrawled on the wall, was the letter *B*.

Targ moved at an easy pace, certain he would find his quarry in the end. There was no need to hurry—the scent was plain, the path easy. He would have the girl and he would have her soon. Anticipation sweetened the savor of the hunt.

He wondered what it was she had that Schlein wanted so badly. He didn't think it was just lust that made the magician so anxious the wench be brought to him. He had seemed frightened. Targ had seen that plainly enough.

There had been rumors of a powerful amulet, he remembered. One of the few guards who could read had caught a glimpse of some sort of journal. It hadn't taken long for those whispers to reach Targ.

Perhaps this female had stolen it? If so, it would not be difficult to get it from her. Targ had always thought he had quite a way with prisoners.

Of course, he had no idea how to use it. But there were many alternatives. One was to hold the girl and the amulet for ransom. Targ would demand heavy payment for their return—much more than any reward Schlein might decide to hand out. Perhaps the Dark Lord himself would be grateful for its return.

Even Targ felt uneasy when he thought of the Dark Lord. But, he reasoned, if the amulet was truly valuable, then the Dark Lord might repay him well for his loyalty. Perhaps he would be elevated to a high station and given an army to command.

For all his powers, the Dark Lord still relied on troops of men and orcs to conquer and pillage. Those who trafficked in the world's goods, whatever their station, could be bribed or bought or tempted. They had desires Targ understood. If what you possessed was truly desired by another, did you not possess that person as well?

Targ laughed aloud. He anticipated great things.

Bith paused to listen. There could be no doubt—she heard water falling. Cheered, she quickened her pace, forcing herself to put more weight on her ankle. Her quest, she felt, was nearing its completion, and she longed for the conclusion. Whether the end was for good or ill mattered less to her than that it be known.

And time was growing short. Schlein must have sent pursuers after her. How long could it take before they found her?

Bith's lip curled in disgust when she thought of the magician. It galled her to flee from the likes of Schlein. The Dreamstone was more powerful than any magic he possessed. Why should she run when she had such a weapon?

She envisioned herself, tall and stately, standing before her cowed enemies. The Dreamstone lay upon her breast, its light so bright it seemed that she bore a burning star. Who could defy her, she who was so complete in beauty and in anger?

It was a compelling vision. Meg's warnings seemed foolish. The sorceress was old, hemmed in by fears and hesitations. *But I am young*, Bith thought, *and unafraid. Why should I discard what has fallen so fortunately into my hands? It's true it's perilous, but all great endeavors entail risk.*

She walked along, entranced by dreams of glory. *Perhaps, given time, I might defeat the Dark Lord himself.* The thought was intoxicating. She saw herself entering the heart of the Dark Lord's realm, banishing shadows with the Dreamstone's searing light.

The Evil Lord would be displaced and, in his stead, she would be a queen. Stern and proud, she would rule with an implacable but just hand.

Perhaps it was fate, and this was her destiny fulfilled. Had she not agonized over and over again about what path should be hers? Perhaps it was she who would free the land of its dark enemy.

Still, doubts nagged at her. Common sense told her that she could not challenge the Dark Lord, that Meg had warned her about the stone, that she was behaving like a fool, that her face was streaked with dirt.

But the voice of common sense was getting weaker.

Schlein stared into space. There was no news. Targ had not returned. The Dreamstone still evaded him. The silence of the caverns oppressed him. Always he pictured himself as being the center of activity.

At his command, armies moved into position, battles were fought, lives were lost. He was the eye of the hurricane— silent, calm, but the heart of a terrible force that revolved around him, doing his will.

Now he felt as if all that had been an illusion. He was abandoned, left behind. Events were proceeding without his knowledge and outside of his control. He had lost his most prized possession and he could not recover it.

His world had been snatched from him, and life was bitter.

The orcs stared at the hole thirty feet above them. "Did they go up there?" one of them asked, pointing. "Could they fly?" another asked, clouting him on the ear.

"Well, then, where did they go?"

"They must have gone off into a side passage. Come on, we'll have to backtrack."

Grumbling, the orcs turned around.

CHAPTER
12

Bith stood on the ledge and looked across at the falls. The water poured over the side, deafening her with its roar. The world receded, fading in the clamor and the mist. She stood alone, with the Dreamstone.

She held the stone up and stared into it. It's heat, coming at her in waves, warmed her cheeks. Again came the sense of falling forward, into a deep pool. Again, she was engulfed in a red wash. Instead of fighting against these sensations she welcomed them. Soon, there would be answers to all her questions.

The dancers swirled before her, draped in silken swathes that caressed her and drew her forward. They were also singing, in sweet, dark voices. Although she could not understand the words, she knew that this mystery, too, would be revealed to her. She would join this chorus.

It came to her that the dance was a ritual, opening gateways to other places, other vistas, and that, given time, she would plumb them all to their depths. Once she knew the intertwining gestures, the complex rhythm, and could join the dancers, worlds within worlds, receding to infinity, would be hers.

Were these dancers once mortals such as herself, who had forsaken all to become one with this encompassing rhythm? How long had they been in this place?

Her questions came faster and faster, tumbling over each other. But she felt herself to be entering a realm of thoughts and events that had no parallel in the world she knew.

Soon, the language she had spoken all her life would be inadequate to frame the strange agonies and grandeurs that would be hers. She must learn another tongue. There would be no sharers from her former life in her new home. All her past would be erased.

Her breath quickened in anticipation. Surely this was her heart's desire fulfilled. Had she not yearned for transcendence, for escape from her own life's vagaries and sordidness? Here was her path to freedom. This was the place of truth, of absolutes, what she had wanted all her life. She was certain she couldn't be wrong.

But first, she must meet the master—he whose pulse was the rhythm that ruled the dancers' steps. It was he who would decide if she was worthy of tutelage, and it was he to whom Bith would offer payment.

That there must be a sacrifice was plain to her. The thought left her untroubled. Certainly, such power and knowledge would be dearly bought. It was only fair. Bith had no qualms about what would be asked of her. All she had, all she was, she would willingly give. Dimly, she remembered a time when she had had hesitations about what would be required of her. Vague warnings slipped faintly through her memory. Had someone once told her it was all lies and deceptions?

Contradictory impulses still plagued her. Her old life still kept a hold on her. That Bith, the old Bith, still wanted to hide her eyes, to flee, to leave this place and return to the safe world she had known. But she was summoned—there could be no doubt. The pull of the Dreamstone was inexorable, undeniable. She could not turn away now. Soon, the old Bith would be dead.

As for what would take her place, she could not yet answer that question

Her fears, she told herself, were those of a weakling who was afraid of the destiny that beckoned so clearly. The warnings she remembered were those of either a liar or a fool. They could be dismissed.

Trepidations were to be discarded. Now that these fears were conquered, and the step taken, there could be no regrets. She saw herself peeling away the layers of being that she had called "Elizebith" like a snake shedding its skin.

She would be newly born, a different creature entirely. The frail woman, the daughter of Morea, the inept sorceress . . . all these identities would be stripped from her willingly—burned away in the master's unending fire.

She was being drawn ever forward, toward the center. As a token, a foretelling of things to come, marvels were revealed to her, sights disclosed, that alternately awed, shocked, disgusted, and aroused her. No matter how extreme the vision, she did not turn away. Her appetite for revelation was enormous.

Strange beings beckoned to her from their various chambers, others ignored her. Each was a monstrosity, a wonder, a glory born in excrement. She hungered to know them all, to feed on their squalor and their brilliance.

She was moving faster. The worlds flashed by her in a blurred progression. She saw briefly, but with total clarity, an enormously fat man, sitting cross-legged on a mat. Collops of flesh hung from his jowls and his sides. His huge belly rested on his knees, and he cuddled it as though it were an animal.

His eyes and mouth were sewn shut with black thread,

but a strange humming sound came from between the pursed lips, and he rocked back and forth in a constant motion. It occurred to Bith that his movements were synchronized with those of the dancers, and also, that despite his blindness, he was well aware of her presence.

The bloated body was covered in pustules. Horrified, she saw one of them bulge and burst. Out of the mess poked the head of a falcon, sharp-beaked and fierce. Its golden eye rolled wildly as it struggled to free itself from its encasement. With a harsh shriek of triumph, it soared into the vastness and disappeared.

What was she to make of it all? How could she explain the hermaphrodite, which flaunted its body in postures of pure sexual display? Or the thousands of tiny, multicolored creatures that formed and reformed themselves into patterns of incredible complexity? Or the sluglike being that crawled along, exuding a sticky, glowing substance that marked out glyphs of mysterious significance?

Her mind was overwhelmed. Sensations she could not describe bombarded her. A moan escaped her lips, part desire, part repugnance. Her body was bathed in sweat.

A dark shape was emerging before her. Her mind denied what her eyes clearly saw. After seeing grotesqueries, the recognizable form was hard to fathom. The familiar was stranger than all the sights she had seen.

It was a black horse galloping toward her. Perhaps it had come to take her to her destination. The long mane and tail flowed in the air, as, swiftly, the animal crossed distances she was unable to measure.

Finally, it stopped before her, pawing the ground, its hooves striking sparks. It was a stallion, massive, powerful, with lathered flanks and flaring nostrils. The red eyes that stared at her had intelligence and awareness. They were what gave the Dreamstone its radiant light. This animal was not a dumb beast—it was more than it seemed. It was the master of the stone.

Obeying an inner compulsion too strong to deny, Bith knelt before it. It became clear to her that she was seeing the expression of an idea, rather than an animal of flesh and blood.

This was wildness, a foreign intelligence, strength, untamed pride, and rampant lust, contained within a shape comprehensible to her eyes. And she realized that all she had seen in this place was but a mask.

Everything here was a living symbol—a hieratic mark that stood for emotions and ideas she could not yet comprehend. The tangible was only a representative of the mysteries it concealed. Flesh was the servant of meaning. Her study here would be to pierce the veils of the flesh and penetrate to the interior.

The master spoke, in a voice that had nothing of the ordinary about it. The words formed in her mind, burning themselves into her consciousness.

"Elizebith, daughter of Morea—thou hast come. I have waited and hungered for thee. Join me, and this realm, and all that it contains shall be thine.

"Thou shalt be purged of all resemblance to humanity. The taint of mortality shall be taken from thee. Thy shape shall be changed, thy memories burned away. This paltry body that imprisons thee shall be discarded. Thou shalt be my victim, my captive, and thou shalt suffer in my flames. My passion shall burn thee. But from the ashes thou shalt be reborn, and rise again as my queen. Do I not offer far more than thou shalt give?

"Look at me, Elizebith. See what awaits thee if thou turn from me."

The voice was commanding. She raised her head and looked into the stallion's eyes. She saw her reflection, young, firm-fleshed. Subtly, the image changed. Her eyes grew harder, and yet sadder, the flesh sagged, just a little, the mouth tightened. It was Morea, or it was herself. How could she tell?

The movement toward decay continued. Intricate lines crept across her face, inscribing tales of regret, anger, and pain. Her cheeks fell in, her eyes dulled, the breasts sagged. She averted her gaze.

"I can save you from this, Elizebith, if you will be mine. Humanity's end is bitter. Join with me, and beauty shall be yours forever. Death shall be banished. Surrender, give yourself to me, and thy reward shall outstrip thy greatest imaginings. My arms shall shelter thee from the common lot of thy kind.

"Thou shalt have power and knowledge beyond all others. All disguises shall fall away, the mysteries cloaked in myth and symbol shall be plain. Thou shalt rule over the world of mortals, and be as far above them as they are to the ants that crawl beneath their feet. All this can I give thee, should thee yield thyself to me. Now speak, and say what is in thy heart."

Bith opened her mouth.

"Bith," Cal shouted. "Where are you?" There was no answer save the unrelenting roar of falling water. A white mist hung in the air. The falls were nearby, although still not visible.

"What if we're too late?" Cal asked. He looked worried.

"We're almost there, Cal. Stay calm," Endril urged him.

"She was ahead of us, this is the only way she could have gone. Why doesn't she answer?"

"Who knows?" Endril said. "Don't jump to conclusions. Bith is a survivor. I know she's alive."

They hurried on. It seemed as if they would never reach

their destination. The sounds, the mist, tantalized without fulfilling. All they wanted was a sight of the falls.

Soon, soon, Cal wished. *Let it be soon*.

It seemed he was walking not through air but a thick soup that held him back and hindered every move. Each step was becoming a struggle. He felt the sweat bead on his brow.

Cal looked over at Endril and Hathor and saw that they too were struggling. Their labored breathing sounded painful. "What is happening to us?" he wondered.

And yet again the air seemed to change, to chill, to wrap them in cold arms. A rank smell permeated the cavern. They stopped.

"Is back?" Hathor asked.

Endril nodded. "Cal," he said softly. "Draw your blade. What does it tell us?"

Cal unsheathed the sword and it glowed a faint blue, a confirmation of their fears. "It's here, but where?" he asked.

Endril shook his head. "How can we tell? We are plagued by things that are not of our world."

Despite, or perhaps because of, his fears, Cal wanted to laugh. He rembered, as a child, playing hide-and-seek with his father. The memory flashed before him as clearly as if it had happened yesterday.

The feelings of anxiety were the same—the tightness in his throat, the anticipation, the pounding of his heart. He pictured himself furtively trying to track his father down, going as quietly as he could, trying to hold his breath so he could make as little noise as possible, biting his lip so he wouldn't giggle.

Sometimes, he would find his father first, and shrieking with delight, hurl himself forward, grasping him around his legs. Sometimes, his father would creep up on him, jumping out from his hiding place with a fierce shout, and Cal would scream and laugh at the same time.

But whether father found son, or the other way around, it always ended the same way. His father picked him up in his strong arms and lifted him high, high over his head. "You're flying Cal," he'd shout. "You're flying like a bird . . . you can see the whole world." And Cal was certain that his father was right.

Now, a part of him badly wanted to believe that his father was waiting for him, and all this would end with Cal high in the air, safe in his father's arms, laughing with pleasure, while the world turned beneath him.

The rest of him said he was acting like a fool of the first water. There was nothing good lying in wait for him in this accursed place. But he was stabbed with a pang for his home and his parents, which was so intense he gasped with pain. He was certain his heart was breaking.

"Cal," Endril said sharply, "look at your sword." The blade had turned a deeper blue. A humming sound was in the air, as if a hive of bees were nearby.

A shape coalesced in the air, billowing and swelling like a sail in the wind. The smell of it was thick, clotted. Their lungs rebelled at taking in the stench. Then it howled. It could have been the wind or the wailing of a spirit lost to all hope. Feelings of desolation and loneliness washed over them. They had never felt so abandoned, so forlorn, in all their lives.

"Papa?" Cal whispered. He was weeping.

Endril's eyes were glazed. Memories engulfed him. He saw his life, and the life of his people, disappearing, vanishing into quaint legends and stories, until their true glory was lost and they were no more than foolish tales to amuse children. His race was dying out, fading into nothingness. All they had striven for was lost.

The world was changing, and leaving him behind. Who would remember the tall, grey-eyed people of the beech trees? Who would sing their songs and praise their deeds? The forests would be destroyed, and the world given over to others, strangers to the ways of the elves.

Grief for the passing of his people ate at Endril's resolve, and his despair deepened. Why was he fighting? What was he fighting against? The inexorable passage of the years? The cycles of ascension, decline, and fall that ruled all the races of the world? It was laughable. He was fighting the very cogs and springs of being.

Perhaps he would return home. He felt the span of his years was fast unraveling. If death was coming, he wanted it to be among his own people, not with strangers, not in this place of cold rock.

Better to be buried beneath the golden leaves that covered the forest floor and to have the rites of his people spoken over his body, as had happened for generations untold. His heart yearned for home and his own kind. Forgiveness awaited him there, and understanding. All would be made clear to him; justice would be done.

Hathor, too, seemed paralyzed. He felt an aching sense of loss that was new to him. He was estranged from his people, a rebel against a way of life that had been followed for uncounted years. Now he wondered if it had been worth it. Why had he left hearth and home? What had he gained?

He stared at his axe. It seemed a foolish toy. He wanted nothing more than to lay it down and leave this place. Home was what he wanted, to return to the familiar places of his childhood. If he could return home, he would never leave it again. His face was wet. Tentatively, he touched his cheeks. Tears.

The shape before them took on more shape, more substance. It was huge—a man, a demon, beautiful, naked, whose long hair was a flame that curled about him in a luxurious inferno. Yellow eyes, cold and mocking, stared at them.

"Weep, mortals," the demon said. "Hast thou not lost all that thou hast fought for? Hast thou not, in thy folly, left behind that which truly mattered, while searching for illusions and follies?"

He laughed, and his hollow voice echoed and reechoed in the caverns till they thought their ears would shatter. "Behold me!" he shouted. "Am I not beautiful in my fire and in my torment? Canst thee hope to find anything so wondrous in thy world, petty and closed? I burn for all eternity. Thy little light shall be extinguished in what is, for me and my kind, but the taking in of a single breath." He gestured to himself, and a shower of sparks illuminated the gloom.

"Go back," he whispered. "I show thee mercy. Return to thy homes. Enjoy them while they are still there. Soon, thy world shall be in the hands of those who do not walk in this plane and who do not think as thee. Then shalt thou truly know grief. I grant thee this respite. Thy time here is wasted. The woman you seek is ours."

Cal lifted his head, and wiped the tears from his eyes. "Elizebith?" he whispered.

"She has joined my brother, he who dwells within the stone, he who obeys the Dark Lord and does his bidding. She is lost to you and your concerns. She shall join him and sit at his right hand. She shall be sister to the fates, and the arbiter of destinies."

"You're lying," Cal said. "Bith would never join forces with you."

The demon's eyes flashed. "I do not bandy words with mortals. Go now, or I shall take thee before the Dark Lord himself. Then shalt thou truly know pain and hopelessness."

Suddenly, shockingly, he tipped back his head and howled like a dog. His sharp teeth glinted in the light he shed.

Endril and Hathor came closer to Cal. "We will not leave without Elizebith," Endril said. "She is as close to us as any kin we may have left behind. I could never rest, knowing I had left her with the likes of you. We know where she is. Let us pass."

The demon hissed like a cat. "The way is barred. None shall pass. Do not come between the Dreamstone and his prey." He lunged at Hathor and his claws raked across the troll's face. Hathor screamed and rolled to the ground, his hands covering his face.

"Cal!" Endril shouted. "Your sword—it is potent against these monsters."

Cal swung his sword with all his might. He felt a mighty power surge along his arm, and he made a fierce and sudden cut. With uncanny swiftness, the demon dodged the blow. He bared his teeth and snarled.

"He fears it," Endril whispered. "There must be powerful spells inscribed on that blade—strong enough to banish this creature whence it came."

The demon wavered, caught between its sworn allegiance to Schlein and its fear of the blade that glowed so brightly. He was bound to Schlein by ties forged in blood, by vows uttered in ceremonies of power, and by the sacrifices Schlein had made to fulfill his part of the bargain. But Schlein was growing weak, and the sword had great potency.

"Quickly," Endril said. "Before it escapes." And then he leapt at the demon. His body passed through the demon's as though it were air. But its incorporeal fire seared him, and he cried out in pain as he fell to the ground. His breath came in ragged gasps.

Cal screamed and swung again. Again came the surge of power and the sword bit into the demon's body, going in up to the hilt. Cal felt resistance as though the blade were sinking into flesh.

The demon howled in agony. Smoke curled up from around the wound. The room smelled as though lightning had struck. And then, the howl turned into a terrible wail and the demon vanished. The wail lingered in the air, fading into nothingness.

Cal staggered and fell to his knees. The sword blade was gone. It had melted in the heat of the demon's body like an icicle thrust into a tub of water. Only the hilt remained. Cal dropped it. His arm felt numb.

Endril crawled over to him. "Well done, Caltus. Truly, you have banished that foul being into the nothingness from which it came."

"Are you all right?" Cal said, barely managing the words.

Endril nodded. He held out his hands, showing the blisters that had risen across them. "I didn't come off too badly," he said. "Praise these sturdy clothes which saved me from a real roasting."

They looked over at Hathor, who was sitting up. Ten red welts were on his face. "Good boy," he said, nodding to Cal. "Nasty thing . . . felt like putting face in cookstove."

"Bith . . ." Cal gasped. They rose and started running down the tunnel, calling her name.

CHAPTER
13

They saw her, perilously balanced on the ledge. She was kneeling and looking up at something. To their eyes, she was alone, but plainly she was bewitched by some sight that had ensnared her. Her hand was cupped as though it held a small object. She paid no attention to their entrance.

Endril motioned for them to stop. "Don't startle her . . . look where she is." They saw that she was right on the edge of the precipice.

"What's wrong with her?" Cal asked.

"She is under an enchantment," Endril said. "I am certain it has something to do with the Dreamstone, but I cannot see it."

"Bith," he called gently. "It's Endril." There was no response. "Can't you hear me?"

Somewhere, Bith knew, someone was speaking. But the words were meaningless. She heard them as a muffled roar, lost in a background of detail that was fast fading to grey. Soon, she would be deaf to the noise and clamor that she had foolishly allowed to take up so much of her life. Now other things concerned her. She was about to make a great commitment. There was no time for nonessentials. She savored the moment.

Motioning the others to hold still, Endril began to creep stealthily toward her. He planned to grab her by the collar and drag her from the edge. If she had the Dreamstone somewhere about her, he would try to find it and throw it over the cliff. What else but the amulet could have brought her to this place? It must be hanging from her neck, invisible, spinning its web, ensnaring Bith with its blandishments.

Targ had trailed them to the waterfall. He had picked up the mingled scents of the troll, the elf, and the man where they joined the female's. He was pleased. They were an excellent quarry. Clearly, they had scaled the wall to get up here. Targ had no doubt his fool troops were wandering the tunnels trying to track a scent they would never find. He didn't mind. When he returned, there would be many opportunities to punish them for their stupidity.

He had seen the encounter with the demon, and his esteem grew. He also was pleased to note that the human had lost his sword and that all three were greatly weakened. He decided that he would attack the troll first. He was the one most heavily armed, and the toughest. Things were going well.

Now he saw the three ranged behind the girl, and the elf moving toward her. The female seemed to be lost in some sort of rapture. He shrugged. She was the least of his worries.

Targ sprang into the room with a roar, leaping at Hathor. Snarling, he pulled the axe from the startled troll and tossed it away. He saw the welts running across Hathor's face and pressed one huge hand across them. Hathor screamed. Targ shoved hard and sent him flying into the cavern wall. Hathor's skull struck the rock with a sharp crack.

Endril sprang to his feet and charged Targ, his dagger drawn. Cal grabbed the orc around the knees and tried to pull his legs out from under him. Targ kicked him in the face.

Endril slashed, parting Targ's leather jerkin, but he never got another chance. Targ grabbed his hand and squeezed. Endril gasped as the blisters broke, and dropped the dagger. Targ picked him up as easily as if the elf were a sack of feathers and hurled him to the ground. Endril moaned once and then lay still.

Throughout all the ruckus, Bith never stirred. She had moved far, far away, and was lost in the glamour of the Dreamstone. Although the world intruded into her meditations, it was shattered and unrecognizable.

The Dreamstone had robbed all earthly forms of meaning and content, and she felt no need for their return. Present time meant nothing; the world meant nothing. Somewhere, something moaned and shouted. It did not matter. It would all fade away soon enough and something else would take its place. Her senses were deserting her, one by one. That too was a matter of indifference. They would be replaced by others, giving her new, undreamt of pleasures and pains.

"Thou shalt not listen, my queen," the master said, in a voice that was almost a purr. "See how the fools wrangle and brawl. Do not let them distract thee. Give but thy word, and thou shalt never be troubled by their noise again. Thou must commit thyself to me. I can do nothing without your consent. Give yourself to me."

Bith stirred uneasily. It seemed she detected fear and unease in her master's statements. Why should that be? Surely an omnipotent being had no need to worry about the actions of mortals. And she was powerless, was she not?

The master seemed to sense her doubt. "It is not for myself that I worry. It is for thee, who are still so vulnerable to the distractions of the world."

Now Bith was certain she sensed disquiet. There was too much wheedling in the voice. It made her pause. What could threaten so powerful an entity?

The babble of noise that surrounded her increased. Fragments of words came to her, and her vision cleared a little. She thought she knew where she was. Someone very far away was calling her name. There was something she had to do. . . .

Targ reached down and grabbed Cal by the nape of the neck. He shook him back and forth the way a terrier does a rat. Then he dropped him onto the ground. Cal landed with a grunt. He struggled to his feet and stood there swaying. Targ laughed and hit him in the stomach.

Cal doubled over and backed away. He couldn't breath. The orc kept his ground, hands on his hips, still laughing uproariously. Then, Cal felt his foot go over the edge of the cliff and he stood swaying, trying to regain his balance.

With a shriek, he fell off.

His hands caught onto the edge, and he hung there. Hundreds of feet below, the river leapt and foamed. Frantically, he dug his boots into the rocky side, trying to find a foothold. There was nothing. The wall was slick and smooth.

Targ peered over the edge. "Hello, little boy. I think I let you stay there till you drop. It's a long way down." Cal tried to haul himself up onto the ground, but Targ made a vicious swipe at him. Startled, Cal dropped back, almost losing his grip.

"Careful, little boy," Targ whispered. "You almost fell." He began pacing back and forth. "I will wait till you die. Then I will take the girl. I think maybe she has something very valuable." He glanced at Cal. "Little boy, you are sweating. Do you know what the little girl has? Tell me, and I might let you live."

"I can't talk like this," Cal gasped. "Let me up and I will tell you."

"Oh, little boy, you must think me very stupid. All the people think the orcs stupid, I know. But that is not so." Targ snarled. "Tell me or die. It does not matter to me. I will find it, no matter what."

Targ paused and a cunning look came over his face. "Remember, if you tell me what and where it is, then I just take it from her. Otherwise, I will have to find it. And I will do it while she is still alive."

Cal was frantic. He didn't think Targ would let him live, no matter what. But his gorge rose when he thought of the orc touching Bith.

His arms were beginning to ache dreadfully and his hands were tired. He knew he couldn't hold on much longer. He was shocked to see how calmly he contemplated his own destruction. Imagination showed him an endless fall, his body turning in the air like a leaf caught in the autumn updraft. The wind would roar in his ears and mingle with the sound of the water below. It occurred to him that Bith's dream was a portent of his death, not hers.

He craned his neck to look at her. She was as still as a statue, spellbound by an enchantment he couldn't comprehend. Her body could have been carved from stone.

It saddened him to leave her without a word. He wanted to rouse her, if only for a moment. If only he could reach her, he might save himself too. With that thought, his terror returned. "Bith," he called. "It's Cal. Princess . . . help me."

Targ stopped pacing. "Little boy, your time is up. Tell

me what I want to know, or die.'' He stood, a hobnailed
boot poised over Cal's aching hands.

Everything happened very fast.

Hathor slowly, quietly, got to his feet. He crouched,
gathering his strength to leap at the orc. A dislodged pebble
rolled down the slope. Targ wheeled around. Hathor sprang
at him. Cal felt his hands slip. ''Bith,'' he screamed, ''help
me!''

A shudder ran through Bith's body. Some urgent appeal
had shaken the very foundations of the Dreamstone's domain. A rupture shattered the perfect geometries of the
crystalline world in which she was encased. Her forsaken
world, her rejected self, reached through the breach to re-
claim her. Her humanity called to her.

The black beast shivered as the underpinnings of its world
were challenged. Bith saw it quaver and break, bursting
from the confines of its restricted shape into an amorphous
cloud of heat and light. Only the eyes remained, burning
red with malice and lust.

''Bith, please, I'm going to fall!'' The cry was human,
filled with terror and despair intensified by the hope that
inspired the call. She wavered, balancing between one world
and another. And then Bith remembered what she had to
do and who she was.

Targ and Hathor rolled over and over on the rocky ground.
They slashed at each other with their fangs, biting wildly,
foam dripping from their mouths. Because of the sloping
ground, they were coming close to the ledge. Neither of
them seemed to care.

Targ managed to roll on top of Hathor and straddle him.
He snapped at the troll's throat. Hathor grabbed the orc's

head in his arms and tried to twist it around and snap the neck.

Targ broke his grip but overbalanced and fell off. Hathor, still on his back, lifted his legs and gave a savage kick. Targ staggered backwards.

Bith bent over and gripped Cal's wrist, pulling him back onto solid ground. "Hello, Cal," she said simply.

"Bith," he gasped. "Are you . . . "

"Excuse me," she interrupted. "I have something I have to do."

Cal watched as she seemed to take something off her neck. Again, she stared into empty space, but with a gaze so intense he was certain she discerned more than he.

"I am Elizebith, daughter of Morea," she stated calmly. "I shall find my own destiny. I am neither montrosity nor goddess nor queen. I am myself. And being myself includes, every once in a while, being a vain little fool." And then she laughed, happily, as one who has freed herself of a great burden. Extending her arm out over the abyss, she opened her hand.

There was a long moment's breathless silence. Everything was still. And then the water erupted into a fury of steam and heat. The river coiled and lashed about like a maddened serpent. The earth heaved.

They heard a scream, and a body hurtled over the cliff and into the water.

"Hathor?" Cal cried.

"Am fine," the troll answered laconically. "Orc is gone." He was bending over Endril, helping him to sit up.

"You mean I missed everything?" the elf asked querulously.

"We've got to get out of here," Cal said. The earth was shuddering beneath their feet. He grabbed Bith's hand. The walls of the cavern began crumbling, and a fountain of water spewed out, rushing to engulf them.

CHAPTER
14

"Wake up! Wake up!"

Bith jerked herself upright. Dumbfounded, she stared about her. She was in Meg's house, sitting on the floor. Cal, Endril, and Hathor were doing the same.

"What is going on? What are we doing here? Was it a dream?" she managed to gasp. But Hathor was bruised and bitten. Ten red welts marked his face. Endril's hands were covered in blisters. Cal moved as if he was stiff and sore.

Meg smiled down at them. "It was a dream, but more than a dream. Your battles were very real, but fought on a plane where I, and certain others, could lend you some aid. Still, the victory belongs to you. We could have done nothing without your strength and courage. Really, all of you are very brave. The danger was great."

Endril stared at her. He thought she seemed even older than before. Her skin had a translucent quality and the sunlight seemed to pass through her. She looked very tired.

"Are you all right?" he asked.

She sighed. "It was a great strain. I begin to think I am too old for this world. It may be time for me to visit other realms. This body irks me."

"It was a dream," Cal said in a wondering voice. "I can't believe it. I thought I was going to die, and all the time it was a dream."

"Cal," Meg said in a severe voice, "I begin to think you are hopeless. What are dreams if not the expression of our secret hearts? They are as real as you; they are a part of you." She bit back a smile. "And if you don't think those bruises you have are real, then I don't know what it would take to convince you."

In a more solemn tone, she said, "The danger you were in was all too immediate. There were times I thought you would be lost forever. Had you three been defeated by Schlein's demon, or you, Bith, been unable to break free of the Dreamstone's spell, you would have wandered, like wraiths, forever. The death of the body and the death of the spirit were both very real possibilities."

She smiled again. "But you have emerged triumphant. The Dreamstone is lost. And you shall be rewarded. Stay with me until you are rested and your wounds have healed. When you leave, it shall be with gifts and honor heaped upon you."

And so they remained in the stone house in the hidden valley until their strength returned. They slept peacefully at night, and, if they had dreams, they could not recall them when they awoke. They did not count the hours or the days.

Sometimes, Bith thought about the Dreamstone, and the mysterious worlds that she had seem within it. She wondered where the stone lay now, what strange waters hid its temptations, its beauty, its obscenity.

Occasionally, especially in the evenings, as the sun sank behind the mountains, and the moon glittered coldly in the twilight sky, she was sad and moody, staying away from her friends to wander outside aimlessly or sit by the window and stare.

Feelings of loss preyed upon her, and she tried desperately to remember the sights she had seen while under the Dreamstone's spell. But they were fading, losing their immediacy and color the way an autumn leaf shrivels and fades when it has fallen from the tree. Soon, instead of marvels there would be only a blank, and a nagging feeling that something was missing.

One day, Meg came to her, and spoke. "I know what you suffer. The worlds which you saw in the stone are there for those who would struggle to attain them. But the Dreamstone would never have given them to you. Its way is to falsely tempt with knowledge it does not truly have.

"You would have been its slave—nothing more. And once you were its captive, it would have continued to taunt you, and your hunger would have been your torment. You would have been trapped in a state of perpetual desire, without the hope of fulfillment.

"Possibility would have been taken from you. There would be no change, no movement, only a never-ending craving, which would drive you to perform the Dreamstone's commands in the hope that you would be given peace. But the Dreamstone has no peace to give."

She laughed. "For all your hatred of Schlein, you may have proven yourself his greatest friend. With his skill, he managed to control the stone, but no one rules the Dreamstone for long. It erodes the will and destroys judgment. Schlein would have ended up its servant, not the other way around."

Bith sighed. "Well, I never thought I'd do him a favor, but he's welcome, I'm sure, for all the thanks he'll give me."

"You must believe me, Bith, when I tell you you've lost

nothing. Instead, you have gained. You have proven the strength of your will and your judgment. And most importantly, you have displayed your wisdom.

"To have rejected your friends in favor of the Dreamstone's blandishments would have been a terrible mistake, but one which many who are older, and supposedly wiser than you, have made. You made what you thought a great sacrifice to save your friends.

"It is not yet time for you to decide which way you shall go. Perhaps, someday, you may dedicate yourself to the art, and eventually, after long ages uncounted, may even become like those you saw in your trance.

"But for now, stay with your friends. Reacquaint yourself with the good things of this world. That is my advice to you. There is much time left before you commit yourself to the path I have taken."

Bith nodded. Then she said, "Meg, how do you know Vili?"

"I am acquainted with many who inhabit those spheres, Vili among them. Not a bad fellow, but, really, so very vain." She shook her head. "Very taken with his position, you know. It is his youth, I suppose. But, he did help your friends, and very pleased he was with himself too, I might add."

"You helped me," Bith said. "That was your voice I heard telling me what a little idiot I was. I never would have gotten to the falls without you."

Meg bowed her head. "I helped, but at the end, only you could save yourself."

On the day they had decided to leave, Meg gave them all gifts of money and rich clothing.

To Endril, she gave a pin, shaped like a beech leaf—its delicate veins were made of purest gold, its body made of silver. "Wear it and remember your home and be comforted," she told him.

To Cal, she gave a shirt of mail, light and flexible yet strong enough to deflect a spear's point or an arrow's barb. "Remember that there is no shame in defense or in turning aside the violence of another instead of engaging it."

To Hathor, she gave a gold chain, from which hung a medallion. It had belonged to an ancient king of his race, and was inscribed with the royal sigil. "Let this speak for you, for you are too humble to speak for yourself."

To Bith, she gave a ruby hanging from a silver chain. "Wear this and remember your courage. Remember too that the paths others have traveled are but possibilities—not destinies. You are yourself."

She bade them farewell, and watched as they mounted their horses and rode away. They turned back once and she was still standing there. They waved. They turned back a second time and she, and the house, were gone.

"The land has changed," Endril said. He pointed overhead and they saw a flock of birds wheeling in the sky. Sometimes they heard a crackle in the brush, as if some small animal was scurrying for cover. Everything was coming back to life. At a high crest, they looked out over the land. There was no sign of the Mistwall.

When they reached Galen's Hearth, they wondered what sort of reception they would receive. Privately, Bith wondered if the mouse was still there. She assumed it was.

They came inside, and everyone's head turned. Galen came toward them, scowling, but then his expression twisted into something grotesque which they found difficult to describe.

"I think he's smiling!" Cal said.

"Well, well," Galen said heartily. "Look who's here!

Have a seat, my masters, and my lady too," he said, ducking
his head at Bith. He swiped at a bench with his dishrag.

"You must really forgive me for being so rude-like to
you the last time you were here. Why, we didn't know who
you was, or what brave deeds you done."

He turned to his other patrons. "These here are the ones
what killed the giants with all the arms."

"Giants?" Bith said, looking at her friends. They simply
returned her bewildered look. "And this lad here," Galen
continued, "is the one what bedded the female monster who
was half-horse, half-woman, and had twelve breasts."
Everyone looked at Cal and cheered.

There was a scrambling, scuffling sound, and someone
got up off the floor and walked unsteadily toward them. It
was John Sillar.

"I told you I'd make you famous," he crowed trium-
phantly. He stood before them, weaving a little. "And it's
glad I am to see you back. It's true that if you'd died, the
tales I told might have been a bit more poignant. Everybody
likes a sad story, don't you know. But I don't begrudge it
to you." He saluted them with his mug of ale, and collapsed
into Cal's lap.

They stood outside in the chilly morning air. "We shall see
each other again soon," Endril said. "Bith and I will meet
you both before much time has passed. She and I will see
the beech forests, while you both revisit the homes of your
people. But our ways do not diverge until we reach the next
town. At least we will ride that far together."

They mounted, and started on their journey, wondering
what awaited each of them at the turning of the road.

About the Author

J.F. Rivkin is the shared pseudonym of two writers who live on opposite sides of the country. They coauthored the first two books of the Silverglass series, *Silverglass* and *Web of Wind*. The next two volumes, *Witch of Rhostshyl* and *Mistress of Ambiguities,* were written by the East Coast J.F. Rivkin, while *The Dreamstone* was written by the West Coast J.F., who is currently writing two books on time-travel and dinosaurs.